Escape to Haven presents a provocative story of a man with a Christian worldview responding to a country moving toward socialism and a country that's the target of terrorism. Rob Gable presents a compelling story of how a retired soldier applies his values and principles to the threats he perceives as being brought about by their elected representatives and terrorists.
—Carl Crackel, International Director of the Road Rider's for Jesus.

ESCAPE TO HAVEN

ONE MAN'S ATTEMPT TO PROTECT HIS
FAMILY FROM A RECKLESS GOVERNMENT

ESCAPE TO HAVEN

For Denny & Shannon,
Enjoy the adventure
Robert N. Gable

ROBERT N. GABLE

TATE PUBLISHING & *Enterprises*

Escapte to Haven
Copyright © 2010 by Robert N. Gable. All rights reserved.

No part of this publication may be reproduced, stored in a retrieval system or transmitted in any way by any means, electronic, mechanical, photocopy, recording or otherwise without the prior permission of the author except as provided by USA copyright law.

Scripture quotations marked (KJV) are taken from the *Holy Bible, King James Version,* Cambridge, 1769. Used by permission. All rights reserved.

This novel is a work of fiction. Names, descriptions, entities, and incidents included in the story are products of the author's imagination. Any resemblance to actual persons, events, and entities is entirely coincidental.

The opinions expressed by the author are not necessarily those of Tate Publishing, LLC.

Published by Tate Publishing & Enterprises, LLC
127 E. Trade Center Terrace | Mustang, Oklahoma 73064 USA
1.888.361.9473 | www.tatepublishing.com

Tate Publishing is committed to excellence in the publishing industry. The company reflects the philosophy established by the founders, based on Psalm 68:11,
"The Lord gave the word and great was the company of those who published it."

Book design copyright © 2010 by Tate Publishing, LLC. All rights reserved.
Cover design by Tyler Evans
Author photograph by David Charles Gable.
Interior design by Stefanie Rooney

Published in the United States of America
ISBN: 978-1-61663-144-4
1. Fiction, Christian, Suspense
2. Fiction, Political
10.03.10

Dedication

For my dad, who saw duty in the Pacific during World War II and Korea, for my mom, and for my wife.

CHAPTER ONE

It had been a downward spiral for years. Finally, the trigger had been pulled. Congress, with the approval of the president, seized ownership of the banks. A rumor quickly started that Congress was going to enact legislation taxing all funds on deposit, on a one-time basis of course, of all of the money invested. This caused a run on the banks. Assets were frozen and Congress approved a hefty one-time tax on all funds whether they were in savings accounts, checking accounts, or individual retirement accounts. It didn't matter. Any money in U.S. controlled banks was subject to the tax.

It had taken a little while for Kent to get used to being called Mr. Davidson. He had been called Sergeant Major Davidson for years. He had enlisted in the army when he was eighteen and became a combat engineer. When he was a staff sergeant, he entered the Special Forces, spending most of his career at

Fort Bragg. Barb had been his high school sweetheart. They married after he completed basic training and the combat engineer course. When he retired from the army after twenty-five years of service, he and Barb remained in their home near Fayetteville, North Carolina. He had started a construction business that had thrived. Barb took care of all of the bookkeeping for the contracting business, placing orders and coordinating the delivery of building materials to job sites. Kent supervised his work crews. Business had been good over the years and had picked up even more since the Defense Base Closure and Realignment Commission had brought growth to Fort Bragg. By local standards, Kent and Barb were wealthy, though you couldn't tell it from the home they lived in or their lifestyle.

Kent had learned the value of a good work ethic from his parents, Pappy and Vera Davidson, who lived in the mountains of North Carolina. They owned and operated a successful bed and breakfast business situated in a beautiful lodge constructed of logs harvested from the property. In addition to the lodge was the farmhouse where Kent's parents lived, bunkhouses for guests and hired help, a mess hall, barns, gristmill, stables, fenced pastures, and a spacious garden.

As a boy, Kent's parents showed him through their personal example the need to purposefully take time to worship God and study his Word. Kent had two brothers. His older brother, Cal, and his wife, Jean, lived on the property with his parents and helped run the place. They used to live in Greensboro where Cal owned and operated a feed store. Cal was about average height and slightly overweight from spending too much time behind the desk and leaving the harder work to his hired help. He was a good-natured person who was normally found with a broad smile on his face. With their parents approaching eighty years old, Cal and Jean sold the store and moved into the lodge to help run the business.

Brad, Kent and Cal's younger brother, had run off to New

York as soon as he graduated from high school. It was there that he expected to find his fortune. He ended up in Washington D. C. working as a staffer for Senator Bailey Beauregard Bates, more commonly known as B. B. Bates. Other than Brad, the Davidson's had been disheartened by the trends they had seen in the country. They were dismayed when prayers were no longer allowed in schools and before sporting events. They were equally affected by the removal of the Ten Commandments from public places. It had even seemed that Christianity was coming under attack. The appointment of liberal judges was bringing about the changing of laws without the benefit of participation by the people's elected representatives. The courts seemed to side more and more with the extreme left-wing agenda.

Kent had suspected that disaster was looming for the country. In addition to turning away from God as a nation, the country was now quickly moving toward socialism. The country's debt was getting out of control. Rather than stimulating the economy by reducing taxes, Congress' solution to balancing the debt was to tax the rich. Congress's answer was always increasing taxes on the rich and then redefining what rich was. The increasing taxes had become a burden that threatened his parents' bed and breakfast business. His parents, with Cal and Jean's help, were doing all they could to keep the business afloat despite the draconian measures of the government.

He and Barb had made numerous trips to the mountains to help his parents and brother improve the property and prepare to survive in isolation from society if the need arose. Kent's parents had firmly told him and Barb that if the economy collapsed and his family needed a place to go, they could escape to Haven. They would always be welcome. His grandmother had come up with the name Haven when Kent's grandparents first bought the property so many years ago. His grandmother thought that the valley was her safe haven where she was protected from the outside world.

Kent hoped to continue working in construction at Fort Bragg, building up a nest egg for the future. He planned to live in Haven someday and knew that there were costs associated with that lifestyle, even with there being no mortgage. Kent's pension would go a long way toward meeting the day-to-day needs. However, a nest egg would be convenient for capital-intensive projects that were expected to arise occasionally.

It had also been arranged that Barb's parents would be welcome in Haven too if need be. They lived just outside of Charlotte. On trips to work in Haven, Kent and Barb would pick up her parents on the way. Due to their age, they only did limited work around the place, spending most of their time relaxing and enjoying the property. God had so blessed the Davidsons; it pleased Pappy and Vera to bring enjoyment to Barb's family. Kent had also talked with his brother Brad about making plans to come to Haven should disaster strike, but he said he didn't think he could deal with the rural life.

Everything that Kent and his parents did in their lives was intended to honor God. They were meticulously honest in all of their business dealings. They were all active in the churches they attended. Above all else, Kent wanted there to be no question that he and his family served the Lord. Consequently, he had become disillusioned with how so many in businesses operated. The bottom line was all that many of them cared about. He was also disillusioned about actions being taken by Congress. Some states in the country were on the brink of bankruptcy. The federal government takeover of ever-increasing portions of the economy would ultimately lead the nation to the same end. The elected representatives seemed motivated by power rather than the good of the people. On the other hand, Kent sought to deal fairly with everyone he came in contact with whether they were subordinates, suppliers, or customers. Integrity and faithfulness to God was what motivated Kent.

When the banks had been taken over by the federal government, everyone wanted their money out and they wanted it out now. Lines had formed, and things had gotten ugly fast around the country. People frantically went from bank to bank and from ATM to ATM, trying to retrieve what cash they could lay their hands on. The National Guard had been called out in many states to restore order. People had become desperate. Thefts of ATM machines became common. Hold ups of any business that had cash were increasing daily. When the banks had closed, businesses would only take cash as payment. They would no longer take credit cards, debit cards, or checks. Employee paychecks that were direct deposit were still being deposited, but employees didn't have access to the money and started demanding cash payment from their employers. There was violence and rioting, particularly in the larger cities. Many businesses had to close their doors. Martial law had been declared in California and New York. The rest of the country was expected to follow the same course soon.

It was obvious to Kent that if the banking system didn't get propped up quickly that he would be out of business. He realized that the movement of goods would come to a standstill. Not only would he be unable to obtain the construction materials for his projects on Fort Bragg, but access to food across the nation would become perilous as well. Food would be scarce, driving prices up in an economy with insufficient cash to operate without the acceptance of checks and credit. Fuel would be nearly impossible to find. This would probably be followed by brownouts or even the complete loss of power in large regions of the country. This would all bring undue hardship and an acceleration of the economic and social breakdown.

That evening Kent sat down to watch the news to see if there had been any improvement in conditions around the nation. As much as he tried not to, Kent couldn't help but be irritated when he saw Senator Bailey Beauregard Bates giving a press conference. The senator was an intimidating man. He stood about six foot two and had a portly stature. He wore expensive clothing and was always accompanied by an entourage of aides and security people giving him a heightened feeling of self-worth.

Kent and Barb couldn't imagine how B. B. could say the things he did with a straight face. It was even harder to think that he could actually believe the things he was saying, they were so outlandish. Tonight he said that the spending recently approved by Congress would bring prosperity to North Carolina. Kent didn't see it that way. He couldn't see how borrowing to spend on short-term projects could help the long-term well-being of the state and its people. Any gains to be derived in the short-term would be more than made up for by the massive debt that would be passed on to future generations. Kent considered it ear candy for the masses. It was what B. B. thought would make an adequate number of people satisfied enough to re-elect him back into office. So far it had been working.

B. B. Bates and Kent had attended the same high school. They both graduated the same year and they both joined the army at the same time. Though they had not been close friends, they had at least been familiar faces as they went through their military training and at their first duty station. Kent had entered the army planning on making it a career. He was proud to serve and proud to wear the uniform every day. B. B. on the other hand had only sought the educational benefits that a tour in the army would offer him. It was also evident that B. B. only strived to achieve acceptable minimum standards. Kent would always do his best no matter how menial the task. Kent had little respect for B. B. in school and had little respect for B. B.'s service both in the military, and now in the United States Senate.

Presently, B. B. was a senior member of the Senate and known for being able to make things happen when there seemed to be no hope. His latest folly resulted from his actions as Chairman of the Senate's Committee on Banking, Housing, and Urban Affairs. Legislation had been passed which resulted in the federal takeover of the banks which directly led to the economic collapse the country was now experiencing. As far as Kent was concerned, it didn't take a degree in economics to see the policy error that had led the nation to the brink of ruin. It was madness to say the least. No matter what spin he put on it, Kent couldn't begin to explain how those in power really thought that these measures were going to help the country. Kent began to wonder if their purpose was somehow sinister. Perhaps they wanted to actually bring about the complete collapse of the nation. *But why*, he wondered.

While B. B. had bided his time during his military tour, Kent had taken college courses at the continuing education center on post to better himself as a person and as a soldier. Kent's most recent success as a contractor working on substantial government contracts had brought Kent to B. B.'s attention. B. B. remembered Kent from high school and the time he had spent with him in the army. B. B. thought that Kent was too much of a choirboy for his taste. Kent's firm was now winning lucrative government contracts for building most of the new infrastructure at Fort Bragg, the home of the XVIII Airborne Corps and the Eighty-second Airborne Division, the U.S. Army Special Operations Command, and the U.S. Army Parachute Team. Despite being a respected fixture in Congress, B. B. resented the success Kent had attained for himself.

Power and recognition were the two things that most motivated Senator Bates. Having these two attributes was more important to B. B. than maintaining the riches he had acquired over the years. However, he didn't expect to see a drain on his wealth. Much of it was safely protected and concealed in offshore accounts. He gave the appearance of being for the common man but lived the life of the wealthy upper-crust aristocracy that he had envied in the past. His position as a U.S. Senator helped propel him into their league. He was comfortable there.

As a long time fixture in the political world, B. B. had developed a network of cronies. They both feared and respected B. B. as a man that could get things done. When he called for a favor, there was no asking for an explanation. When B. B. had some problematic issue to attend to, he would normally start by calling Alexander Booker. Booker was a well-placed agent with the Internal Revenue Service, giving him ready access to a plethora of valuable and often incriminating information that could be used as leverage against B. B.'s adversaries. Agent Booker could also put pressure on B. B.'s opponents by virtue of Booker's position. With B. B.'s backing, Agent Booker had developed a network of support of his own that enabled him to reach even into the unseemly side of the world.

Agent Booker was a wiry little man with thick glasses. He didn't look intimidating; however, he got people's attention when he showed his credentials. The IRS seemed to make most people uncomfortable. Though working out of Raleigh, Booker's influence comfortably reached from Virginia to South Carolina.

As a consequence of actions initiated by B. B. and passed by Congress, the exchange of goods and services quickly came to a halt following the closing of the banks. Food was no longer being delivered to grocery stores. The basic necessities of life could no longer be obtained. That applied to building materials as well. Out of necessity Kent suspended his construction projects at Fort Bragg and quickly arranged for him and Barb to pick up her parents on the way to Haven. He also called his dad to let him know they were on their way and hoped to be there before the end of the day.

The people of the country had immediately lost what little trust they had left in financial institutions. Following the run on the banks, all financial assets had been frozen. Checks were not being accepted as forms of payment. Credit card companies changed credit limits to zero so that cash could not be withdrawn. Overnight, cash had become the only acceptable form of payment. Fortunately, Kent had previously kept a supply of cash on hand for just such a contingency.

It had all begun in earnest several months ago. On the eve of the inauguration Kent and Barb had hosted a social at their home for the Sunday school class that they attended. They were all concerned about the proposals of the incoming president and had concerns about the country's future. Anticipating that the government would bring about the collapse of the country's economy and encourage the terrorists to attack again on U.S. soil, Kent proposed that they establish a safe place to escape to when the time came. He had received permission from his father to use their place up in the mountains for that purpose. His family was also interested in the proposal, and his friends were intrigued. Some people considered him a right-wing enthusiast based upon what he was proposing.

After months of working in Haven with his parents and with the help of friends and others that wanted to be included should the need arise, the time had come. Kent had started bringing his construction projects on Fort Bragg to an end. Some had to be left unfinished due to the unavailability of supplies and materials. During the most recent trips he had made to Haven, Kent had shuttled to the property most of the personal belongings that he and Barb wanted to keep. There was no hope of selling their home near Fayetteville until the country's economy stabilized. Until then, Kent asked some neighbors to keep an eye on his place and the things he was compelled to leave behind. Despite all of the preparations, getting to Haven was more difficult than had been anticipated.

There had been no problem picking up Barb's parents. It was after that that the challenges began. The National Guard had been instructed to set up roadblocks at key points on main roads and limit travel. It wasn't really clear why movement had been restricted, but it created problems nonetheless. Maps had to be referred to or local people asked how to bypass the checkpoints so that they could get to Haven. It seemed that the country had gone crazy.

It had just gotten dark. The National Guard had stopped Kent and his passengers at a checkpoint and sent them back the way they had come. They were getting concerned on how they were going to reach Haven. They pulled off the main road to stop and study the map and try to figure out how they would continue. As Kent was studying the map, they were all startled when they heard a light tap on the car window. They all looked up with a start and saw a tall, lean black man, probably about seventy years old. He had a shotgun gently lying in the crook of his right arm. Kent apprehensively lowered the window.

"You all having problems? You need any help?" the man asked.

Kent looked up. "Actually, we do. We're not broke down. We were turned back by the National Guard and don't know how to get where we're going."

"Where you goin'?" he asked.

Kent angled the map toward the man and pointed to where Haven was located, though it didn't say Haven on the map. "Here. It's not far, but I don't know how best to get there from here. Do you have any suggestions?"

"First of all, I would suggest you folks get off the road. It's not safe to be out during the day anymore, let alone after dark. Why don't you come and stay with me and my wife and get started again in the light of day?"

"That's very generous of you, but we wouldn't want to put you to any trouble," Kent replied.

Barb was concerned about their predicament. "Kent, I think it might be a good idea to take this man's advice."

"I'm JM Washington. People around here just call me JM," the man said.

Barb looked at Kent and said firmly, "Let's take JM's advice and get started again in the morning."

"JM, my name is Kent. This is my wife, Barb, and her parents. I guess you've got four guests for the night."

"Okay, nice to meet you all," JM said. He pointed to a spot down the road and asked, "See that dirt path to the left just ahead?"

"Yes, I see it," Kent responded.

JM pointed to the same spot. He then pointed back off the road. "Turn in there and follow it 'till you see the house. Then drive around to the back and park by my truck. I'll be along in a minute. I want to walk back and check a couple of places on the fence line. I'll see you there." JM started walking away from the road. Following him was a big, brown dog.

Kent followed the instructions and turned left down a bumpy dirt path that led to a fair-sized farmhouse. He followed the well-worn path around the right side of the house and pulled up beside the truck. Kent felt uneasy. "I hope this is a good idea. We don't know this man."

"He seemed like a down to earth person to me," Barb said.

"I agree," Barb's father stated. "I feel as though he has our best interests in mind."

"Okay. Let's just wait here until he—" Kent spotted JM. "There he is."

JM motioned with his hand for them to follow. They all got out of the car and followed him to the back door. The dog stood by JM, wagging his tail, watching them approach the house.

"Wait here for just a minute. I want to tell the misses that we have company." JM had hardly finished his sentence before he had stepped into the house. He was gone only a moment when a short, stout black lady quickly came to the door. She had a big smile on her face and enthusiastically said, "Come on in. Come on in. My name's Hazel. It's not often we have company."

They followed her into the kitchen, where she asked them to sit at a large table.

Hazel said, "It's a pleasure to meet you. I didn't know we were having company, but I could offer you some cornbread and sweet milk until I could get something more ready. How about some fried eggs? We've got plenty of eggs."

"Thank you," Kent replied. "However, we stopped for supper a little ways back."

"Well, how about some sweat tea and a piece of pecan pie?" Hazel asked. "I just baked it this afternoon. The pecans are from the tree in the backyard."

"Thank you. That would be nice," Barb replied. It's very thoughtful of you to take us in like this, Hazel."

"We couldn't leave you out on the road, could we?" Hazel commented. "Things have changed around here lately. It used to be such a quiet and peaceful community, but lately people have started breaking into homes, trying to find food for themselves and their families. And of course, there are those that use our present troubles as an excuse to bring hardship on others. I wouldn't give you a nickel for any of 'em."

Barb asked, "How are you two getting along now?"

"JM makes a point to be seen walking around the place with his shotgun. He continues to wave, nod his head, and give a smile as people drive by. I think those that want to bring trouble have decided that there are easier places to take their mess."

"How about shopping? What do you do about that now, if you don't mind my asking?"

"We've pretty well got what we need to get by with for a

while. I've stayed with the old ways and have continued to can food and make pickles, jams, jellies, and the like. JM tends to the smokehouse and keeps us in meat, and we have chickens for eggs. We're pretty self-sufficient. We'll be able to make it if these troubles can get worked out after a while."

JM had entered the room and joined in the conversation. "Yes. We can hold out for a while, but I don't know how long this will go on. I've never seen anything like it."

Kent responded, "Neither have we."

Kent, Barb, and her parents were enjoying the company and refreshments when JM looked at Kent with a serious look on his face. "I saw on the map where you're headed, but I don't understand why. There's a small town nearby, but why are you going there?"

"Many years ago my grandparents bought a valley outside of that little town you saw on the map. Now my brother Cal and his wife, Jean, help my parents run a bed and breakfast called Haven and educate local school children that come out on field trips about gardening and taking care of animals. In fact, my mom and dad established a nonprofit educational organization which provides funding for the educational aspects of their operations. Since the banks collapsed, they've stopped receiving paying guests at the bed and breakfast and have geared up to help take care of family and friends. Of course we're all going to be expected to fill in for the hired help that they had to let go. They're down to a skeleton crew. We're going to all work together to operate as much as possible as a self-sustained community."

Kent explained to JM all of the development that had taken place to include construction of the buildings, providing for the electrical needs and a lot of the other work that had gotten Haven to where it is today. At various points in the story, JM would nod in agreement or at least that he understood what was being explained. He didn't interrupt. His wife had sat down in a chair in the corner and started mending a shirt. A little later, she set her work in her lap and gently rocked in her chair. It actually looked like her mind had wandered off to another place or time.

When Kent had finished, JM spoke up. "It sounds like you've made a place kind of like what we have here, except on a larger scale—something we could never have accomplished here alone, but with the same idea in mind with what the misses and I have tried to do with our lives. Why are you really doing this? Is it to escape the woes of our country so to speak, or is it bigger than that? Are you making a new life of sorts for yourselves?"

"The basis for what we are doing is to provide a safe place to live despite the damage being done to our country by our elected representatives. Whether there is a greater purpose or not, I don't really know."

JM then looked at Barb. "Ma'am, do you think you'll enjoy moving to a rural environment like where you're goin' in Haven?"

"You know, I do." Barb replied. "We know that the family and friends that will come are mostly believers in our Lord Jesus Christ. It will be nice to live among people with similar beliefs for a change."

"We're God fearing people too." JM then asked Barb's parents, "And how about you two, what do you think Haven holds for you?"

Barb's mother answered. "For me, it's a place where I believe I'll be able to more fully enjoy and appreciate what God has given us. I'm thankful for my family. I'm also looking forward to enjoying the company of fellow believers in Christ. I understand that most of the residents of Haven are well founded in their beliefs. We won't all be of the same denomination, but most of us believe that we are sinners saved by the grace of God and the sacrifice of Jesus Christ. I'm hoping that Haven will be a place where we'll feel at the center of God's will. It seems that God has been leading us all in this journey so far, even though there have been a few bumps along the way."

Then Kent answered. "It has seemed like a miraculous endeavor. If I had tried to imagine something like this, I would have never believed it possible. I too have felt led along this journey. Before the idea of moving to Haven came up, I was running a construction company, putting up buildings on Fort Bragg. It was very profitable, and we were reaping the rewards of our labor. And even though I know I am saved, I felt that there was something more important that I could be doing with my life. I hadn't planned or even thought about moving to Haven so soon, but now I believe that it's something that God put before me. It took some soul searching. It took some time away from my work and ultimately has taken me completely away from it. Barb and I have spent most of our spare time in recent months helping get Haven situated. I did get satisfaction from the work I had been doing at Fort Bragg, but I believe that God has told me it's time to move on to more important things in life. It seems that the next phase of our life's journey begins in Haven. Whether that's the last stop before Heaven or not is in God's hands."

JM and his wife were moved by what they had just heard. JM asked, "How many people will there be living in Haven?"

"We've been planning based upon there being no more than thirty or so people," Kent replied. "However, we have set things up so we can expand to eighty if need be."

JM knew it was getting late. "I guess you'll need to carry some things in for the night. Would you like a hand bringing them in?"

"No thank you. There are just a couple of small bags we'll need. I'll go get them and be right back."

Kent went to the car and got what they would need for the night. They were then shown where their rooms were. Kent and Barb were directly across the hall from Barb's parents.

Kent tried placing a call to Haven but couldn't get a signal on his cell phone. Barb didn't have service on hers either. He then asked JM if he could try calling on his phone to let his parents and brother know they'd be arriving later than expected. JM informed him that the phone lines had been out of service for the past couple of days. Kent knew that his family would be worried sick. After visiting with JM and Hazel a while longer, they all went to bed.

Paul and Sarah Williams were the first to arrive in Haven following the economic collapse. Like Kent, Paul and his wife, Sarah, had also spent a career in the military. Paul had also been in Special Forces for most of his career. He had seen combat serving as a medic in Vietnam and in Iraq during Operation Desert Storm. Through his association with soldiers still serving he intimately learned of the devastating effects that Islamic terrorism could unleash. Since retiring he and Sarah spent most of their time in the quiet solitude of their farm, which was situated on a dirt road over a mile from the hard top. Sarah enjoyed helping with the garden and putting food away for the winter. However, they each contracted a few hours a week as nurses at Womack Army Medical Center on Fort Bragg.

There had been nothing for Paul to go back to in Puerto Rico where he'd grown up. His parents had passed away years ago, and he'd lost touch with any family members that remained. What he had especially liked about living around Fort Bragg was the acceptance people had toward people from other parts of the country and the world. He'd rarely experienced problems when he was out alone or with Sarah.

Chi Le had taken the American name Sarah to make things easier for her and Paul. They met in Vietnam. Sarah had married Paul there and had escaped with many of her countrymen during the evacuation that accompanied the fall of Saigon in 1975. Paul had come up with the money required to get her to the United States. They eventually reunited in Washington State when Paul was assigned to Madigan Army Medical Center just north of Fort Lewis, Washington. They finally ended up at Fort Bragg, with Paul working at Womack Army Medical Center. Over the years, Paul had helped Sarah master her English-speaking skills and encouraged her to enroll in college.

Sarah had always been interested in Paul's work and decided to become a nurse. She had a natural gift for the math and science involved. It was comprehension of lectures in the early years of her college education that were the challenge. With the permission of her instructors, she would tape the lectures and play the parts back for Paul that she couldn't understand. Paul had always been patient during the process and could not have been more supportive. It had been especially hard juggling her schoolwork, responsibilities at home, and raising two boys. She had taken a light school load in the beginning and picked it up after the boys began school. She tried to always be home when the boys left for school in the mornings and when they came home in the afternoons. Now they were both grown and serving in the military. The oldest was in the army serving as a military intelligence sergeant in Afghanistan. Much to his father's dismay, the youngest had joined the marines and was serving at an embassy in the Middle East. Paul and Sarah were proud of both their sons. They just wished that they were able to see them more often.

It hadn't been long since Paul and Sarah had made the transition to farming from their life in the military. Paul had thought that he would miss being in the army and had not been in a hurry to retire. The time had just arrived. He really thought that he would miss serving on active duty but had found that the challenges of getting his farm up and running were a lot more work than even he had envisioned. The contracting work at the hospital also assisted with the transition. Oh, he didn't regret the decision to retire to the farm; in fact, he relished it. Paul had been offered lucrative contracting positions paying six-figure salaries, but it would have required him leaving Sarah at home and deploying into the box in the Middle East for months at a time. That's not what Paul and Sarah had sacrificed for all of the years they had spent in the army. Though Sarah had not actually been in the army, she felt like she was as a dependent of a Special Forces soldier.

Cal was the first to speak with them when they arrived. Cal had known they would be coming but didn't realize that they would be coming today. It didn't present a problem though. Paul and Sarah brought with them skills and abilities that would be a valuable asset to Haven whenever they arrived.

The next to arrive was Barb's sister, Sally Franks. After going to college after high school Sally had become a teacher. That had been thirty years ago. She had taught second grade and really enjoyed the children in her class. She had decided to go ahead and retire largely due to changes within the school system. She had to watch what she said about religious issues. She had to be careful about handling disciplinary problems, and there was no backup or support from the administration in the school where she taught. Sally was also disheartened that many parents had no ambition for their children or for themselves other than to exist off welfare programs. For some, this had gone on for generations.

Sally had also recently gone through an ugly divorce. She had come to rely on her sister for emotional support through her difficult time. It had not been easy adjusting to life alone again. She was thankful that there were no children involved. She had witnessed the devastating effects that separations and divorce had on the children in her classroom. She had a lot of sympathy for the kids that were from broken homes and that were having difficulties adjusting to their new living arrangements.

It was well past the time that Kent was expected in Haven. His parents were starting to get worried. Cal said he'd try and reach Kent and find out where they were. Cal went to the office and tried calling Kent's cell phone. Kent didn't answer, so he left a message. He then tried Barb's cell phone, but again, no answer. It was unusual for Kent and Barb not to pick up, especially when they could see on the caller ID that it was him calling. He kept trying about every fifteen minutes, but to no avail.

A little after dark a car pulled up with a family of five. Cal had never heard of the Martin family, two adults and three fairly small children. They claimed to be friends of Kent. Not being able to reach Kent and not knowing what else to do, he had them move into the vacant bunk house. Mr. Martin said he'd been laid off from work awhile back due to the economic collapse of the country and had just had his home foreclosed. They had nowhere else to go. On top of that, they hadn't had anything to eat since the day before.

Cal told his parents about the surprise visitors. His mother said that he had done the right thing taking them in like he did. As Christians, they couldn't turn away a family in need. She asked him if he and Jean would arrange for the family to have something to eat, even if it was only peanut butter and jelly sandwiches.

Before he'd had time to prepare the sandwiches, the Rivera family showed up with a similar story to that of the Martins. They didn't claim to be invited guests of anyone. They just needed help. While Cal met the Riveras and got them settled, Jean continued preparing the sandwiches. They were a family of three: him, his wife, and a teenage boy. There were plenty of beds available, but no vacant bunkhouses. The guests were going to have to share the space. There were two spacious bunkhouses that could easily accommodate twenty people per building and more if needed. These had mostly been used when youth groups had visited their bed and breakfast: the boys in one and the girls in the other.

Cal's mother was pleased that he had been so hospitable to the people that arrived. Cal, on the other hand, was becoming concerned about what would happen if people kept showing up like this. They had made preparations, but not for a lot of unexpected guests.

As bedtime approached, Cal and Jean tried not to let on how concerned they were. Kent was never late for anything. He would have called if he could. Cal and Jean had heard on the news about the National Guard roadblocks. The country had become filled with desperate people trying to survive in a world where they could no longer rely on being able to buy food. Cal and Jean told his parents that they just figured they got delayed somewhere and had to check into a motel. Truthfully, Jean feared that they had been involved in an accident, maybe killed. Cal was afraid he'd never see his brother again. Then the phone rang. Cal received a call from his dad, "Cal, your mom's fallen down the steps. I need help."

Cal was afraid for his mother. She had become less mobile recently. "I'll be right over, Dad." As soon as he hung up, he hollered, "Jean, call 911. Mom's fallen down the stairs," as he ran toward the front door of the lodge he ran for the farmhouse where his mother and father lived which was a couple of hundred yards away.

CHAPTER TWO

Kent was up early the next morning and met JM in the kitchen. JM invited Kent outside to walk around and talk for a few minutes so they could speak privately.

"I was interested about what you told the misses and me about Haven last night. I know this is none of my business, and I won't take offense if you don't want to answer, but I was wondering what it would cost to come and stay in Haven for a while."

"No offense taken. My mom and dad charged a fee when they were running a bed and breakfast, but the bed and breakfast has closed down. Right now we just want a few likeminded people living in Haven. It'll take a lot of work to keep things going and provide adequately for a good number of people. Naturally, it took a substantial amount of money to get things up and running, and members of the family along with a few others have invested in the place. On the other hand, some of those coming to Haven have made little or no financial contribution. What everyone is expected to bring is a willingness to contribute their knowledge, skills, and abilities for the betterment of the overall community."

"I see," JM thoughtfully responded.

Kent continued. "We realize that this arrangement sounds like a commune, but we prefer to think of it as cooperative living, really like a big family. When you have a society with as many people as we have in North Carolina, cooperative living isn't practical. Capitalism is the most productive, fair, and equitable road to take. However, when only a few people are involved, it takes everyone pitching in together to make for a good standard of living. Understand that we realize that not everyone has the same ability. We just ask for an equal effort." Kent paused for a moment and then turned and looked directly at JM. "JM, if you don't mind, I'd like to ask you a question."

"I'm listening," JM answered.

Kent asked, "What is it that you've work for in life?"

"Mostly I guess it would be taking care of my family. Now don't get me wrong, the misses and I are God-fearing people like you are. We go to services every week and study God's Word regularly; but here on earth, as the man of the house, I've got to do my best to provide for my family. You've met the misses. Our kids are grown and have moved off and started their own lives. We see them every few years."

"So having a big house is not important?" Kent asked.

"Not really. We've been comfortable here. The landlord's been good to us by not raising the rent a lot and letting us pay a few days late when we're short of cash."

Kent then asked, "How about a big, fancy car? Would you say that's important to you?"

"See that old pickup? It gets us where we need to go as well as any car would."

"I see, JM. Is there anything else you wanted to ask me about?"

"It depended on your answer to my first question."

Kent asked again, "Okay, then is there anything else you want to ask?"

"I'd like to know if there's room for an old farm couple like us for a while. I was really exaggerating a bit about how well we are doing. The truth be known, things are getting real hard here. It's always been hard work, but I don't know how much longer I can really hold on with the way things are going. I had a lot of hope in things to come during the last election; but looking back, I don't know what I was really expecting. Things just aren't working out like I thought they would."

"Sure," Kent said in a positive, upbeat manner. "There's room, but this is a big decision. It's something you only heard about last night. I told you quite a bit about Haven. I can see from looking around your place here that you and Hazel would have a lot to offer, but I wouldn't want you to jump into anything you would later regret."

"Is there anyone there like us?" JM suspected he and his wife might not be welcomed due to their race. Where he lived, white people went to a white church and black people went to a black church. It was hard to say why, but that's just how it was.

Kent thoughtfully looked at JM and replied, "We've only met; but from what I gather, you two are one of a kind."

"You know what I mean," JM said. "Are there any black people?"

Kent looked at JM and seriously stated, "Well then, no. At present, there are not any blacks like you and Hazel that have become a part of Haven. There's one man from Puerto Rico, and his wife is from Vietnam. I think you'd find in Haven that the color of a person's skin is not important. We're all children of God."

"Okay. I'm still interested," JM stated with conviction.

Kent asked, "JM, have you discussed this with your wife at all?"

JM nodded. "She was saying before we fell asleep last night about how wonderful Haven sounded and how it would be nice to live in a community of God-fearing people. She thought that Haven sounded like heaven on earth. I agreed with what she was saying."

Kent stated, "We were planning on leaving early, but it wouldn't hurt anything to discuss this together for a while."

"How about we talk more after breakfast?" JM suggested.

"Sounds good."

The two of them continued to walk, making some small talk on the way back to the house.

When JM and Kent went back inside, Barb and Hazel were working together preparing breakfast. Hazel had said no thank you to the offer of help, but Barb wouldn't take no for an answer. Breakfast consisted of pancakes, grits, smoked country ham, and coffee. Barb's parents came downstairs just as breakfast was ready to be served. JM said grace. Then they all enjoyed breakfast together. They visited like old friends.

After breakfast, Kent said to Hazel, "I understand that you might like to see some pictures we have of Haven."

"Oh yes, I would," Hazel eagerly answered.

Kent proceeded to show an aerial picture of the property to give a frame of reference and then pictures of the farmhouse, lodge, bunkhouses, and gristmill. He then showed pictures of the living accommodations for the residents. He explained how all the living areas had been furnished about like what she saw in the picture.

Hazel said, "Oh, I'd love to live somewhere like that if we could afford it."

JM answered, "Hazel, that's not a problem. There's no cost to move in or to stay other than helping with the work to keep the place up and produce the food. We do that kind of work now."

Hazel looked at Kent with a questioning look. "Is that right?"

"Yes, ma'am. That's how things work in Haven. In fact, there's no money involved among the residents. When it's time to eat, we go to the dining room and eat together. If you need any type of supply, you go to the storage area that's located in a cavern behind the lodge. All of our basic needs are met."

Hazel couldn't believe what she was hearing. "How can that be? I don't see how you can do that."

Barb placed her hand gently on Hazel's forearm and said, "Hazel, we've been working to make a place where we can all live in peace despite what may be going on in the rest of the state, or in the country for that matter. Those who were able provided the resources for the construction of the buildings and provided the supplies to stock the storage area. Please understand that there will be good times at Haven but there's also going to be a lot of hard work. There are not enough supplies to last the community forever. We'll all have to work. But know this; entry into Haven is based on your desire to work with others to meet the needs of the community. This is different than the way we are used to living."

"I see," Hazel responded.

JM asked, "How do we sign up?"

Kent replied, "You don't have to sign up. Just come with us. We'll go to Haven together. You'll be all right."

JM stated, "We'd have to bring our animals. We have a couple of barn cats. You met our dog, Pooch. We've got a couple of dozen chickens and so forth. Would they be able to come?"

"We've never addressed a policy on pets. I'm surprised that never came up. I think your barn cats would earn their keep, and Pooch seems harmless enough. The farm animals are no problem. How would you get them all there?" Kent asked.

"We didn't walk back behind the barn. I've got an old stock trailer that I can pull with my truck. We can put a few personal belongings in the bed of the truck and all of the animals and poultry in the trailer."

"How long would it take you to get your things together?" Kent asked.

JM looked over to Hazel. She replied, "I'd like to have the rest of today to think things over about what to take if that would be possible. I know that it will take JM a while to get ready, and I know we wouldn't want to be on the road after dark. I think we could be ready tomorrow morning."

Kent looked over at Barb and her parents, "How about we stay here for another day and leave tomorrow about this time?"

Barb and her parents each nodded in agreement.

"I'll try to call Haven and let them know we're going to be arriving with another couple and hope to arrive tomorrow.

After breakfast, Kent unsuccessfully tried to contact Haven. The rest of the day he spent helping JM go through his things as JM decided on what to take and what to leave. Barb and her parents spent the day assisting Hazel. JM and Hazel knew that their space would be limited and took care to take only things that would be beneficial to their new way of life or those that had sentimental value.

At the close of a busy day, they all sat around the supper table, finishing off what the ladies had prepared. Barb asked Hazel, "So, are you excited, scared, do you have any second thoughts?"

"I think that, most of all, I'm hopeful. I'm hoping that life will be meaningful and that we will fit into life in Haven. Don't get me wrong. I've loved my life here with JM," she said, smiling over at her husband, "but I would really like to have a sense of community, to enjoy the company of others. I really liked the way you described the socials you have on Sunday afternoons. It reminds me of when I was a child. We'd pack up a box dinner and go to church. In the afternoon, we would visit the other people from church out on the churchyard. We'd sing praises to God, we'd play games, and we'd have fun. We'd have another worship service in the evening and go home tired but happy from a time of fellowship. I haven't known that in a long time."

"Hazel, we haven't lived there yet ourselves," Barb stated. "We know how nice it is though. We have the same hopes that you will like it too."

After cleaning up and a little more visiting, they all started getting ready for bed. It would be a busy day tomorrow.

Cal was thankful that the ambulance had arrived so quickly the night before. As far as they were from town, he thought it would take much longer. Normally he would have put his mother in the car and drove her to the hospital, but she had hit her head; she was dazed and lying at the bottom of the stairs when he had rushed into the house. She was unable to move. Cal was afraid that if he moved her without medical supervision he might make things worse. The twenty-minute wait seemed like an eternity at the time.

His dad had ridden in the ambulance with his mother to the hospital. He and Jean drove in their pickup. It was a miracle that his mother hadn't broken any bones. She was bruised. The bump on her head, however, was much more serious. The doctor insisted that his mother stay overnight for observation. Pappy wanted to stay in the room with Vera. Cal and Jean wanted him to come home and sleep in his own bed, but they figured he wouldn't be doing much sleeping anyway and relented. The doctor said it would be all right.

The next morning Cal called his mother's room at the hospital. His dad answered. He was told that mom seemed groggy, and the doctors hadn't been in yet this morning. Pappy told Cal to go about his business and keep trying to reach

Kent. When Vera was lucid, she was asking about Kent. Over breakfast Cal and Jean prayed that his mom would be all right and Kent and the others would arrive safely.

About midmorning John Turner arrived in Haven. John had been one of the attorneys at the law firm that did the legal services for Kent's construction business. He had also provided some legal advice to him and his parents over the years concerning their bed and breakfast business.

For John, as well as other people tuned into what was actually going on in the country and around the world and had the foresight to take proactive measures, the idea of settling in a place like Haven was enticing. John had been considering the prospect of early retirement and had been planning for it for several years. He had envisioned retiring to the country to get away from the congestion of the city. Haven sounded like a provocative prospect. Though he realized that he would be providing legal services to the residents of Haven, his primary responsibilities would be much more varied and to his liking. He had decided to take Kent up on his standing offer to come and be a part of Haven.

Cal had been told by one of the remaining farmhands that John had arrived and wanted to talk to him. He found him in the dining room, sat down, and joined him for lunch. "I'd heard you arrived. Did you have any trouble getting here?"

John answered, "We had to backtrack and find an alternate route a couple of times. Other than that, it wasn't too bad."

John's wife excused herself and joined Jean on the front porch.

"John," Cal said, "I was wanting to ask what you thought about the idea of having a talk with each adult that ends up coming to Haven and determine if there are any legal matters they need to tend to right away."

John asked, "Any specific type of matters you have in mind?"

"Sure." Cal had been asked about some personal matters from some of the residents and wanted to help take care of their concerns right away. "I know that we have all agreed that we need to follow the laws of the land. Even though our country is in chaos, the laws are still in effect; and there could be problems later if we were found to be ignoring them."

John suggested, "I could help them with getting their mail forwarded, updating their wills and powers of attorney, and help change where pensions and social security funds are directed so that all will be set when money starts flowing again, as well as any other legal concerns they might have."

Cal asked, "How about I ask Jean to post a signup roster with times and dates so that everyone who wants to consult with you can?"

"Sure, that sounds good," John replied.

Then Cal added, "Also, we could make an announcement at dinner when most everyone is here, encouraging them to sign up."

"That sounds great," John stated. "I'll consider that my mission for as long as it takes. How about after that? I don't see myself practicing law here in Haven as a primary duty."

Cal asked, "Have you thought about what you would like to do?"

"Yes, I have," John said. "Perhaps I could help with keeping the records for Haven and make sure that we have everything that would be required for an audit of the tax-exempt status and that everything is in order from our end for the business of running Haven as well. That may take quite a bit of time at first, at least until things become routine."

Cal agreed. "That sounds like it would be a good place to start. I believe that Barb will appreciate your help in that area. Kent, Barb, and her parents haven't arrived yet. I'm starting to get concerned. They were expected to arrive yesterday."

John had seen the problems on the roads. He said, "Well,

I wouldn't panic yet. Something could have come up, and you know how hard it is to get a phone connection of any type now."

Cal said, "No. I'm not panicked yet. Just a healthy dose of concern."

After a moment of quiet, John asked, "Overall, how have things been going during the last few days?"

Cal tilted his head slightly as if in deep thought and then replied, "I'm pleased that they have gone as well as they have. We've had more people arrive than we were expecting, but I think we'll be able to adjust in a timely manner."

John then asked, "What's been the best part of your experience in Haven?"

Cal answered, "In my opinion, it's the freedom. For example, not having to concern myself with what things cost. I know that sounds odd. Of course we have to concern ourselves with what things cost, but we have become pretty self-sufficient. I like not having to worry about whether or not I have enough cash in my wallet, or will I get an order filled on time for example. There's more flexibility. I'm not distracted by all of those types of matters. Jean and I have had a lot more time for each other. Life seems to have slowed down to where we can take time to enjoy the sunset. We can enjoy a leisurely evening taking in a view of the heavens, which we hadn't really seen in years. It's what I picture when I read in the Bible about the peace of the Holy Spirit. It's a lot easier to feel that peace here."

John then asked, "What's been the hardest part?"

Cal gave another thoughtful look and paused again before answering. "For me, I think it's the feeling of responsibility. I have been trying to make sure that everyone is assigned work that is fulfilling for them while still getting everything done. I want everyone to experience the peace that Jean and I do. That requires carefully considering the needs of everyone that lives here. I've had to make some adjustments here and there. Sometimes it has turned out that someone has taken on a responsibility that they thought they would enjoy to find that they really didn't. The reality is not always the same as the dream. We've worked through those kinds of issues together. I think the hardest part for some is the change in mindset required to live here. Before coming here pride of ownership was a key ingredient in many people's lives. However, in one sense, we don't own anything; but in another, we share in owning everything. Sure, my mom and dad actually own the property in a legal sense. But they treat everyone as if they belong. It's a hard concept to get your mind around. It seems to be working for the most part. The mindset that we have to develop here is pride of community. I don't think it would be possible for this concept to work in a community much larger than we have here. With the number we have, you can still get a sense of being an integral part of something bigger than yourself."

"That's interesting," John replied. "I think that your observations just might help me better understand what living here is like. Anyway, I'm glad to hear that things have worked out so well for you and Jean. I'm looking forward to meeting with the others and assisting them with their legal matters. It sounds like that's something that needs to be done. Most will probably be happy to get that done and put those matters behind them.

John, I'm glad you and your wife are here. When you're done with lunch, Jean will show you where you can meet with the others if you think you need some privacy while discussing their personal matters. I've got to start making my rounds."

"Thanks, Cal. It's great to see you. And thanks for sharing your experiences in Haven with me."

"Any time. I'll look forward to hearing about your impressions after you've been here awhile," Cal said.

After lunch Pappy called Cal and said that Vera was ready to be discharged. They'd done all that they could do for her physically. When Cal and Jean had arrived at the hospital to pick her up, they were both taken aback by how she had appeared to age overnight. The fall had taken a lot out of her and seemed to have taken some of her cognitive abilities as well. The doctor hoped that she would return to normal over time.

When they arrived home, Cal and Jean converted a room off the side of the kitchen into a bedroom so Vera wouldn't have to climb the stairs anymore. She said it wasn't necessary, but Pappy agreed that the stairs were getting difficult for both of them. Pappy said he'd like to have the bedroom right by the kitchen.

Cal had continued trying to reach his brother throughout the day and decided to try one last time before going to bed, but he didn't have much hope. It was ringing as before. Any moment Cal expected it to go to the automatic message. Instead he heard his brother's voice, "Cal, I can't believe the phone is actually working."

"Where are you," Cal said with tears in his eyes. "We've all been very worried. Are you okay?"

"We're okay. Right before dark we were turned back by the National Guard. I pulled off to check my map and ended up meeting a nice couple that would like to join us. I think they'll be a great addition to Haven."

"That sounds great. I'm so relieved. When do you think you'll be arriving?" Cal asked.

"I'm guessing a little after two tomorrow afternoon," Kent said.

"Okay, I'll go and let everyone know that you all are okay. Kent, I'm sure glad to hear your voice. See you tomorrow."

"See you tomorrow, Cal. Thanks."

Cal had thought it best to not worry his brother about the fall their mother had taken. He would bring it up when he arrived.

Even though they were leaving in a few minutes, probably to never come back, Hazel insisted on cleaning and straightening up the kitchen. She said the man they rented the place from had always been good to them and that she wanted to do right by him. They were paid up through the end of the month and had until then to make a decision if they wanted to come back or not. They'd still be expected to give thirty days' notice and pay the next month's rent. That gave them a little over two weeks to change their minds if things didn't look like they were going to work out like they hoped.

JM and Kent finished getting the animals loaded up. Catching the barn cats had turned out to be the hardest part. Finally, everything was set, and everyone went out to get ready to leave. JM put his arm around Hazel's shoulders as they looked at the house they'd lived in for so long and just gazed for a long while contemplating their future. Hazel wiped the side of her eyes with a tissue and told JM she was ready. JM and Hazel got in the truck and would lead the way since JM knew the roads best. Kent, Barb, and her parents would follow, giving JM and Hazel a good lead in case something fell out of their truck or trailer.

When they got within a mile of Haven, JM pulled over. They had arranged for Kent to be in the lead as they approached Haven's security gate. Beside the gate was the guard shack, which was well constructed so as to withstand gunfire. Over the gate was a sign that read, "Welcome to Haven." When Kent got even with the gate, he stopped and spoke to the guard. The guard had been on one of his construction crews and knew Kent well. Kent let him know that the vehicle behind him was with them. Then they drove in. Kent led them to the barn so that they could tend to the animals first.

From the garden, Paul and Kent's dad had seen them coming and walked over in time to meet them as they got out of their vehicles. As he approached, Pappy gave them a big smile and walked up to Kent. "We've been worried about you all son. We were expecting you a couple of days ago and were afraid something had happened."

"Well, something did happen," Kent said. "We got turned back at one of the National Guard road blocks. We were lucky enough to meet up with these fine folks. Let me introduce you to JM and his wife, Hazel."

"It's nice to meet you both." Pappy reached out and shook JM's hand.

"And this is my dad. He goes by Pappy," Kent said.

"It's nice to meet you too," JM said. He was surprised at the warm welcome. It seemed genuine.

"Yes. It's nice to meet you, Mr. Pappy," Hazel said.

"No need to call me mister. It's just Pappy."

"Then it's nice to meet you, Pappy," Hazel answered again.

Kent said to his dad, "I assured JM that we'd find a place for his animals. I hope I didn't speak out of turn."

"Don't worry, son," his dad said reassuringly. "It looks like he's got some fine animals and poultry."

It didn't take long to get the animals and poultry unloaded and placed in their new homes. It was time to introduce JM and Hazel to the others. Pappy let JM know that his truck and trailer were fine by the barn if he'd like to leave them there. Barb's parents, Barb, and Hazel all got into the car and drove over to the lodge. Kent and JM walked over. Once they were all assembled at the lodge Kent led the way into the reception area and introduced JM and Hazel to his sister-in-law, Jean, and explained that he'd told them that they would be welcomed as new members of Haven.

Jean was surprised but didn't let it show. What surprised her was their age. She was wondering what they were going to do in Haven. It didn't take long to find out. They all sat in the reception area. Cal walked in just in time to participate in the conversation. He let them know he was very relieved to see them and told Kent about their mother's fall. They all visited for a while as they learned the vast experience that JM and Hazel had concerning the old ways. JM had been a mechanic in his younger years and had been farming and gardening most of his life. And, despite Hazel's age, her fingers were nimble with a needle and thread and she could operate the sewing machine that she had brought as well as most anyone could.

While Kent had been making the introductions, Barb had taken her parents up to their room in the lodge to get them situated. When Kent had the opportunity to slip away, he went over to check on his mother. He too was surprised at how she seemed to have aged since he saw her a few weeks ago. He was also concerned about her slightly diminished mental capacity. She was glad he was finally home.

The country was in chaos, but Haven was now assembled for their adventure in community living, tucked safely away from the troubles facing the country.

CHAPTER THREE

Once on site, Kent didn't waste any time getting to work. First, he and Barb had a lengthy meeting with Cal and Jean to get up-to-date on what the current situation was in Haven. Cal didn't mind keeping the place running for a while. However, both Cal and Jean felt a bit overwhelmed with the business end of keeping the place going. They were both glad that Kent and Barb had arrived. The meeting included topics on logistics, supplies, health, morale, welfare, operations, and the list continued. There were no illusions that the transition would be easy for everyone. It was decided that the initial emphasis at this point would be on the people who now lived in Haven. Not only did their physical needs have to be met, but their emotional ones as well. It was going to be difficult to adjust to a complete shake up in their day-to-day way of living. At least for now, there would be no going to the mall, the restaurant, or wherever else everyone was used to going. Even though the grounds were spacious and esthetically pleasing, some would undoubtedly get cabin fever.

Also of a big concern to Cal was security in Haven. The situation with the country was having an adverse affect regionally. Cal thought it would be a good time to beef up security. There was presently good security at the primary access point to the grounds. However, Cal thought it would be a good idea to have regular patrols check the perimeter of the property to make sure that Haven wasn't compromised. He reminded Kent about the stockpile of weapons and ammunition in storage and that there were a number of good shots among the residents. Several of them had taken advantage of target shooting as a part of the Sunday afternoon activities. Kent thought the patrols were an excellent suggestion and assured Cal that he would work something out soon.

One day Kent stopped by to visit his brother Cal who was at work in the cavern. Kent was surprised to hear a clanging sound in the back and went into one of the shafts a ways to see what was causing the racket. Kent found Cal hitting the wall with a pick, like he was prospecting. Cal turned, startled at Kent's appearance, but quickly regained his composure.

Kent asked, "Cal, what are you up to back here, trying to find some gold or something?"

"If any is to be found," Cal replied. "Kent, do you remember when we were kids, Mom and Dad would take us to a gem mine each year?"

"Sure I remember," Kent answered.

"We'd go to the mine, pay an entry fee, and dig as long as dad would let us. To me, it was kind of like going fishing. Remember the saying how a bad day fishin' is better than a good day workin'? It's kind of like that. I could dig and dig. You didn't have the same fascination with it that I did. You'd get bored and go off and do something with Mom."

"Yeah," Kent answered. "I didn't see much point in spending so much time at it."

Cal continued, "You're right. I didn't ever find much. But boy was it exciting when I found something that looked interesting. So when I take a break here, I get to go back to my childhood, looking for the secrets that the ground holds."

"You know, people could get the wrong idea and think you're trying to find gold for yourself. Let's say you did find some. Then what would you do?"

"Kent, I hope you know me well enough to know that I would consider it our property, not just mine. How about if I agree to let you know if I find anything worthwhile right away?"

"Okay. Okay," Kent said. "You've got my complete confidence. All I ask is that you lock up when you go on break and keep your mining activities to yourself. I know I have no business telling you this you being my big brother and all, but if you do get into a deposit of gold, then we'll get some people to help you. You wouldn't want to keep all of the fun to yourself, would you?"

Cal nodded and said, "You've got a deal."

As he was returning to the lodge, Kent started thinking about his wife and sister-in-law. Kent was thankful that Barb's sister, Sally, had decided to join them in Haven after all. She had gone through so much with the divorce. And her and Barb had become so close lately. Anyway, she would be a great asset with organizing the Sunday socials and Friday evening entertainment.

Sally had originally planned to work a while longer, teaching in the public schools. However, since she had reached her minimum retirement age, she went ahead and took it so that she could be a part of Haven.

They all agreed that it was essential that everyone who had not already consulted with John about their personal affairs, who wanted to, do so soon. It was important to those who had taken the lead in Haven that everything and everyone was kept on the up and up with regard to meeting all legal requirements. John had spoken to more than half the residents so far. Others hadn't been so quick to respond to the offer of his assistance.

It was clear that contact with the outside world, which had been so easy before the troubles of the country started, was now difficult at best. John would continually monitor access to the outside whenever opportunities presented themselves and process the matters that needed to be taken care of for the residents of Haven when it became possible.

Next, they agreed that a priority was the assignment of duties among the residents. It was a fine balancing act to have people with enough to keep them occupied, but not so overburdened as to feel like they were being given more than their fair share. Of course, there were those like Paul who worked as long as there was still light and was driven with a sense of accomplishment in all that he did. Those who had been in Haven awhile had already adapted to the work environment and what it entailed. The new arrivals were to be guided toward duties based on their knowledge, skills, and abilities. If they decided the work they'd agreed to do was something they didn't find interesting after all, they were encouraged to discuss the matter with Cal to ultimately find a position that would be both satisfying to them and beneficial to the community.

To start getting to know some of the residents John Turner and his wife sat with Paul and Sarah during lunch. The conversation turned to the time that Paul served in the army. Sarah explained, "Paul and I have had a lot of experience with chaotic times. While Paul was on the front lines, I was at home with the kids, trying to get all of the information I could by listening to the news. I've spent many sleepless nights worrying about Paul and the soldiers he served with. Many had been guests in our home. Some didn't make it back from deployments. The downfall with our country's economy and the battle against our country by terrorists is not of our choosing, but we can't run away from or ignore it either. It's coming at us and coming at us fast. There's no way we, as a people, can live in safety as long as the ideals of the Islamic terrorists survive, and it's nearly impossible to kill an idea. Paul and I have had many discussions about what to do. We've even considered pulling up stakes and moving to another country. However, Islamic terrorism is a worldwide problem. We just don't hear as much about the terror attacks outside of our country and Europe."

"I agree," John said.

Since moving to the farm after Paul's retirement from the army, Sarah had come to more fully appreciate the satisfaction that comes from hard work. "Paul and I have really enjoyed going back to the basics of living. It seems to me that things are more real when you're working with your hands in the earth. You see more of what God has so richly blessed us with. I can't imagine living in an urban setting anymore where you'd have to make an effort to find a place to walk that isn't pavement or concrete."

It didn't take long for the trouble in Haven to begin. Apparently some of the residents were expecting a lot more varied menu, something like you'd get at a buffet restaurant. What was actually offered was a family-style, take it or leave it meal.

The cooks were having difficulty preparing meals to accommodate the right number of people. For example, they had prepared food for twenty, but by the time the meal was served another family had shown up, making the serving sizes accordingly lean. The night Kent arrived with the others the food that had been prepared was exceptionally insufficient. When the prepared food ran out, residents were given a choice: cold cut sandwiches or peanut butter and jelly.

Life in Haven didn't turn out to be what some of the residents expected. They had anticipated living in one of the spacious rooms of the lodge and being treated like they were the guests of the bed and breakfast. Well, that's how it worked for paying guests when Haven was being run as a bed and breakfast, but not now. Times had changed. Now it was a community of people living communally. Paul didn't like to think of it in those terms. He preferred to call it cooperative living. Either way, it was a lot of work for those that decided to stay and be a part of the community.

Then there was the issue of housing. Some of the residents didn't think it was fair that the best rooms went to the closest family members while some of the larger families bunked together in common areas in the bunkhouses. Kent pointed out that other than their labor to help get the work done, their food and housing were being provided for free. They had a choice. Kent didn't like having to be so blunt, but he pointed out that they didn't have to stay in Haven if they didn't want to. Kent figured that after a few days things would settle down and get to a sense of normalcy.

Kent was quickly getting up to speed on the situation in Haven when he met again with Cal and Jean. He wanted to find out about the overall operations of Haven from their perspectives.

Cal explained that several residents wanted refrigerators in their living quarters, but the energy requirements were prohibitive. The energy generated on site wouldn't support the increased demand. It was much more efficient to have things that required cooling to be stored together. There was a walk-in cooler in the kitchen and a small refrigerator in the first aid room for medical supplies that required refrigeration. Finally, there was a refrigerator in their parents' farmhouse. Of course it was decided that they deserved this accommodation due to their generous contribution of the land that they all resided on. Heating and cooling was the other area that Cal addressed. Much of the heating was done with a centrally located wood furnace. With the availability of timber on the property, wood was easy to acquire. As long as the hydraulically operated wood splitter and chain saws were operational, staying warm was not a lot of work.

More challenging was the cooling. Cal explained how the air conditioning had been accomplished by diverting cool air from the cavern into the lodge. The air was then dried using industrial dehumidifiers. It was the most feasible approach to cooling the large facility that they were able to find. As for the farmhouse, cooling was accomplished with window units in the hottest part of the day. However, the house was situated under some nice shade trees and had been built to take advantage of the cool breezes that typically blew in during the morning and evening. The trickiest part of energy utilization was providing enough electricity to use the woodworking and other electrical equipment. This was alleviated by carefully scheduling the times that the equipment was used to coincide with the times of lower energy use within the community.

Jean explained about the social interactions among the residents. She explained that those over fifty years of age or so were adapting the best to the changes that life in Haven presented. For example, most in that age group didn't miss watching the amount of TV they had been used to. In fact, they actually enjoyed the time that was opened up to them for leisure activities such as reading, sitting on the porch in the evening, walking the grounds, fishing, and the like. The younger residents seemed restless. Some had handheld portable video games and listened to music on MP3s. They were able to recharge their players each night in the outlets. They seemed to resent the little amount of time they were able to use the Internet and the fact that it wasn't even available most of the time now that the country's economy had collapsed. They made a point to schedule everyone who wanted some time on the Internet when the system was up and running. It was frustrating for those who were computer junkies before arriving at Haven. The encouraging part of this though was that the ones who had been here the longest seemed to be filling their time with other meaningful activities. Some were even showing an interest in learning some of the skills that made Haven run. Some of the children would go and help in the garden or with the animals without being asked. They looked for something to do that they enjoyed, and Paul was very willing to accommodate their desires.

Later in the day after getting back to the mundane office work that awaited him, Kent was pleased to see his brother enter. "Hi Cal, how are things going?"

"Mostly good," Cal answered.

"What's the part that's not good?" Kent asked.

"As you know, several of our residents have children, and we haven't been able to get the bus from the public schools to start coming here yet to pick them up. They're also saying they don't have it in their budget to send a bus way out here every day. They said we'd have to submit a request in writing for next year's budget if we want them to be picked up here."

"You know, I can see where they're coming from even if their decision is wrong. I think we might be able to take care of this problem for ourselves. Let me look into it, and I'll get back with you soon," Kent said.

"All right, I'll tell the families we'll have an answer shortly. Thanks, Kent. See you later."

It had been a busy day on the hill. B. B. had rushed into the Senate chamber to cast a critical vote and then to an important luncheon with one of his key contributors. When he finally returned to his office, one of his staffers let him know that Agent Booker had been trying to reach him all day. He had just called again and was on the line holding. B. B. was curious about what could be so important, so he accepted the call.

"Agent Booker," the voice on the line said.

"Alexander, it's so nice to speak with you," B. B. said in his typical condescending way. "What do I owe the pleasure of your call?"

Agent Booker was excited about the information he had to share, "Senator, I've got something I thought you'd want to hear about right away."

"I'm listening," B. B. replied.

"It's about Mr. Davidson," Agent Booker said.

"Would that happen to be Mr. Kent Davidson, Alexander?" B. B. asked.

"That's right. Kent Davidson."

"Well out with it then," B. B. firmly stated. He did not like this little man but didn't want to be outright rude with him. He did provide some valuable information from time to time and could get things done when needed.

"Davidson's stopped work at Fort Bragg. His construction crews have stopped working completely," Agent Booker said.

"I'm not surprised. Transportation has come to a standstill. He probably can't get the construction materials he needs."

"There's more, Senator," Agent Booker said with a smile. "Mr. Davidson has moved his family up to the mountains and has moved in with his parents."

"So he's taking a little vacation, what's the big news?" B. B. asked.

"Quite a few people have gone there with him. It seems that they're setting up a survivalist group of some kind."

"Now that's interesting," B. B. replied.

"I've got a friend of mine who's moved onto the property and is living there with them. He's going to keep me posted on what's going on," Agent Booker added.

"Good initiative, Alexander. Keep me posted on what you hear." B. B. hung up the receiver. He thought, *I wonder what Kent's really up to. We'll see.*

It didn't take long to locate Barb. She was working at the reception desk helping one of the residents. As soon as Kent had the chance to speak with her, he explained the problem with getting the children to school. Barb suggested that her sister, Sally, might enjoy home schooling them here in Haven and suggested Kent speak to her about it.

Kent then found Sally who was working in the kitchen. He walked over and asked her for a few minutes of her time. "Sure," she replied.

"Cal mentioned to me that we've not been able to arrange for a bus to come and take the kids to school. I know you have had experience with the public education system. I was wondering if you might have a suggestion on how to proceed."

"Do we really want to send the children to public schools?" Sally asked.

"With all the changes that have come about over the last few years, I guess not" Kent answered. "But the children need an education. In fact, it's required by law."

"We could set up classes here and home school them. I believe we've got the resources," Sally stated.

"We'd need someone to take charge," Kent replied. "You know, look into the requirements, getting the materials, setting up the classes, and the like."

"I'd enjoy doing that," Sally eagerly stated.

"Barb thought you might like to," Kent said.

"Then why didn't you come right out and ask me about it?" Sally asked.

"I didn't want you to feel pressured into taking on a responsibility you didn't want. Having retired from teaching, you might have had enough of it and want to do something else."

"I loved teaching," Sally said. "I just didn't love teaching in the public schools when I decided to retire. This will be completely different. There won't be any problem if we pray in school and read scriptures from the Bible. We can teach the basics and morality. That's what is missing in the schools now."

"Amen to that, Sally," Kent said in total agreement. "So you'll start setting it up?"

"I'll start as soon as I finish up with my kitchen responsibilities," Sally answered.

"Great, I'll give Cal the good news so that he can let the families with children know. Thank you for agreeing to do this."

"It will be my pleasure," Sally said.

"I hate to ask, but the families will probably want to know when we will start."

"Tell them Monday. I'll get some volunteers to help, and we'll start while I continue to research and work out the basics. I'll contact the Board of Education and make sure we do everything in compliance with state requirements."

"Okay," Kent said. "I'll let Cal know to tell them we'll start Monday. Thanks again."

When Paul and Sarah were needed for their medical talents, they made themselves available. Otherwise you could find them working in the garden and fields. They both enjoyed the simple life and appreciated the beauty of what God had created. The next morning they went out to the garden to pick some carrots. The cook and her crew for the day were going to start canning, and the carrots were ready. When they arrived at the garden, they discovered that a whole row had been pulled up and were missing along with some of the other produce that was ready for harvest. They were very upset and went straight to Kent to tell him about it.

"A whole row of carrots missing and more, what are we going to do," Sarah said, disappointment clearly on her face.

"Could one of the residents have taken them?" Kent asked.

"I don't see why they would," Paul answered. "If they wanted carrots, they'd just pull up one or two to eat on the spot. I can't imagine that anyone here would pull up a whole row."

"You're right. Well, Cal and I were just talking about increasing security. I guess we'll need to get serious about it and start now."

"If someone can sneak on the property and steal our food, who knows what else they can get away with," Paul added.

Knowing Paul was also a retired Special Forces noncommissioned officer, Kent asked, "Do you have any suggestions concerning how we should provide for the overall security of Haven?"

Paul responded, "The main entrance is pretty well covered. We just need a way for the guard up front to quickly and reliably call for help if needed. I think that if we provide an audible signal device in addition to the land line, such as a field phone with a line to your office, it should suffice."

Kent continued the questioning on security. "How about any of the other areas around the property? Cal suggested some regular patrols be established. What do you think about that idea?"

"We've got the manpower to do that now," Paul answered. "I think that would be a great. We'd want to set up teams to reconnoiter the perimeter at random times just in case there is anyone or a group of people planning to do us harm."

"Do you have a recommendation on how we could accomplish that?" Kent asked.

Paul answered, "We sure don't want to use the vehicles. First, the terrain is too rough in several places. And second, we need to minimize the use of fuel."

"How about we send them out on horseback?" Kent said. "Maybe we could use JM's mule too."

Paul replied, "That would work. We already have to feed them, and they would move quietly through the property while reconnoitering."

Kent asked, "Do you think the team should be armed?"

"I sure do," Paul answered.

Kent wasn't excited about weapons being carried around the property. He asked, "What would you suggest they carry, the lighter or heavier-caliber weapons?"

Paul said, "I would suggest they carry twenty-two-caliber rifles. If the worst comes, they would not be the primary line of defense. If there were a sign of any trouble, I would have them hightail it to the lodge and notify the others. We need to have plans worked out in that eventuality so that everyone knows what to do. I would even go so far as to suggest we do some practice drills from time to time so that it becomes routine."

"That's a good point," Kent noted. "Paul, I know you're busy, but it would be a big help for me if you would work up a draft security implementation plan. I think we need to get on this as soon as we can."

Paul agreed, said he'd work up a detailed proposal, and figured he could have something by the next day.

Kent then asked if there were any other concerns that Paul had. "You know, with the pets that some of the people brought with them, we could have a big problem brewing. Some of the animals haven't been fixed. We could have a population explosion."

"How would you suggest we handle that?" Kent asked.

"We need to have the dogs and cats given rabies shots if they haven't been and have them spayed and neutered. Several already are, but we need to make sure they all are." Paul emphasized the all. "They'll be better behaved animals, and we won't find ourselves with the decision of using more and more food to feed them or putting them down."

"I know you two aren't veterinarians, but I wondered if this is something that the two of you could help take care of. Any ideas?"

Paul answered, "I wouldn't be comfortable doing it myself."

"Neither would I," Sarah chimed in.

Paul added, "However, I do know a person at the health clinic who's got a cousin that could. We would have to pay him somehow, perhaps barter for some produce, but he could do it with our help. I could talk to him the next time I'm on duty at the clinic."

"Great. Let me know what you find out," Kent said. "Now, how are things going with regard to the health of the residents?"

Sarah responded, "We are available on an on-call basis.

We've been able to take care of most of the problems so far. There's a doctor at the clinic that works closely with us on medical issues that are beyond our abilities, such as some of the diagnosis and providing prescription medications. It would be handy to have a doctor at Haven, but this is the next best thing. I think he admires what we are doing here, so he makes the extra effort on our behalf."

"Yes," Paul added. "We've only had one resident that had to be evacuated. He had a minor heart attack and was taken to the county hospital. He was in the hospital for five days but is back and doing fine now."

"I'm glad to hear that," Kent said.

After a few more comments, the last meeting of the day ended. Kent had his work cut out for him taking care of a few loose ends.

It had been a long day, but Kent wanted to see how his mother was doing, so he went down to the farmhouse. His dad was fine, but his mother seemed to be declining even further. Though she had gotten a good bill of health overall from the doctor, she obviously wasn't herself. He discussed the matter with his dad, and they both agreed that she needed to go back to the doctor. Kent told his dad that he'd call and make the arrangements and be over for them first thing in the morning after breakfast the next day.

As agreed, Kent arrived early in the morning to take his mother to the doctor. His dad helped him get her to the car, and they drove up to the clinic. Kent's wife had agreed to stay behind and work with Cal and Jean to troubleshoot any problems that might come up. As they rode to the clinic, Kent was distressed at learning exactly how much more his mother had declined in just a few days.

Once they arrived at the doctor's office, the receptionist was concerned by her appearance and rushed Kent's mother into the doctor's office. After a brief examination, he suggested that Kent take her back to the hospital. She needed to be admitted to the hospital again. So they all piled back into the car and drove to the hospital. Things didn't go so quickly there. Kent's father was sitting by his mother, comforting her. Kent was pacing back and forth. He checked with the reception area. The nurse assured him that his mother would be seen soon. Kent had always hated going to hospitals.

A nurse stepped out from behind a set of double doors and called, "Vera Davidson."

"Right here," Kent said as he hurried over to help his dad get his mother up and into the examination room. Kent was asked to stay in the waiting area.

About twenty minutes later, a doctor came out and called his name. The doctor said, "I'm sorry to inform you that you're mother has congestive heart failure, in addition to the cognitive issues that she has been experiencing. Her breathing is labored. She has been placed on oxygen and made as comfortable as possible. She's been moved to the third floor, room 305, and your father is there with her now. You're welcome to go up and see her."

At the end of the day, Kent and his father reluctantly left Vera at the hospital and returned home. The next morning Kent dropped his father off at the hospital to spend the day with Vera. Kent assured his dad that he or someone else would be for him late in the afternoon and to call if he wanted to come home sooner.

CHAPTER FOUR

Kent had worked through the issues that had come up during the initial discussions he had held with his brother and sister-in-law. There continued to be limited access to the outside community. They kept up-to-date on state, national, and world events by way of TV and radio most of the time. Occasionally, those forms of media were down for days at a time, and they would keep up with the shortwave radio that Cal operated. Several of the residents would join Cal when the shortwave radio needed to be used. It was an item of interest to some and just something different to do for others.

One morning, around 10:00 a.m., Kent received a call on the landline informing him that there was someone at the front gate that wanted to see the person in charge. Kent really thought of Haven as a community of the residents, but it fell on him to respond; so with some trepidation, he headed for the front gate.

"Agent Booker, Internal Revenue Service. I've got some matters to discuss with you."

"Certainly," Kent replied. "Let's go to what I use as my office. If you don't mind, I'd like John Turner to join us. He is an attorney. I can have him join us right away."

Agent Booker seemed to be a short-tempered person. He curtly replied, "All right. I'll wait, but this had better not take long."

As promised, John joined them within moments of arriving in Kent's office. Kent introduced them.

"John, this is Agent Booker with the IRS."

"Good morning," Agent Booker stated rather coldly.

"Good morning," John answered. John was used to dealing with the starched shirt bureaucrat types.

"This is a serious matter that I'm here to discuss with you," Agent Booker said earnestly. "There has been an accusation that you folks are not in compliance with the Internal Revenue Code of our country and are actively taking measures to conceal income that should otherwise be taxed."

"So, who made the complaint?" John asked.

"It wouldn't matter. I don't have that information. The names of complainants are expunged before being sent to the field for investigation. I'm sure you understand."

"All right then," Kent said. "We're listening."

With a firm voice, Agent Booker said, "The accusation specifically indicates that there is substantial income derived from the premises directly and or in the form of barter. I am compelled to determine the validity of the accusation and make what recommendations I deem appropriate to my supervisor."

Kent leaned back in his chair slightly as he listened to the back and forth between John and Agent Booker.

John asked Agent Booker, "What can we do to assist you in your quest, no, I mean your obligated duty?"

Agent Booker was obviously not happy with John's comment. He spoke in the same abrupt manner, "I'll need access to all of your financial records and will need to interview a number of the people who reside here."

Kent replied, "That's not a problem. John will lay out our records for you. In the meantime, perhaps you'd like to begin with the interviews this afternoon and start on the review of the records first thing in the morning, if that's satisfactory?"

"That will be fine," Agent Booker said in a matter of fact tone.

Kent asked Agent Booker, "Will you need accommodations for the evening?"

"No. That won't be necessary," Agent Booker answered. "I've made arrangements to stay at the motel in town."

"Then who would you like to start the interview process with?" Kent asked.

Looking at Kent, Agent Booker said, "I might as well start with you, in private of course, unless John will be serving as your attorney."

"In private will be fine," Kent answered.

John stood up and slowly walked out of the room.

Kent looked directly into the agent's eyes and said, "All right, Agent Booker. You've got my undivided attention. How may I help you?"

"You seem to be the person in charge here. What compensation do you receive for conducting your responsibilities?" Agent Booker asked.

"What do you mean what compensation do I receive?" Kent replied.

Agent Booker carried an air of superiority about him. He explained, "Payment, of course, or bartered exchange for services rendered."

Kent spoke in a tone of condescension, "Apparently you haven't been informed as to the nature of our living arrangements here."

"I've done some research through the state records and have learned that there are two corporations involved: one that owns the real property, and the other that operates an education operation through the bed and breakfast business."

Kent said, "Well, that was the case until recently. Yes, you're right that there is a corporation that owns the real property. The property has been leased to us, the residents, for one dollar a year. However, we were compelled to suspend the other operations recently due to the economic collapse of our country. Now the residents are in a survival mode. We work together to accomplish what needs to be done such as raise food and maintain the premises and equipment for example."

Agent Booker continued, "That's where the government's concern comes in. Let's talk about the person or people in charge of the farming part of your operation."

"That would be Paul," Kent said.

Agent Booker continued the questioning, "What does he receive in exchange for his service? I would imagine that he receives room and board and cooking benefits. It's bartering one service for another."

Kent sighed. "I don't see it that way at all. Most of the residents in Haven have worked with Paul in the garden. When there are labor-intensive projects, all of us who can pitch in to help. We shift our efforts from one area to another and cooperatively get things done. I don't think you'll find anyone here that thinks about things the way you are suggesting."

Now Agent Booker was condescending. "It doesn't really matter what they say. It matters on what you are doing and for what quid pro quo. I'll have to interview several people to determine how things do in fact operate here."

"That's your prerogative, but I think it's a big waste of your time," Kent said.

Agent Booker replied, "I'll be the judge of that. I'd like to talk with the person that is the supervisor of your agricultural department."

Kent explained, "We don't have an agricultural department. Like I said, we're just a group of people who live here together."

"Call him what you will," Agent Booker stated as if irritated. "I'd like to talk with him. I believe you referred to him as Paul."

Kent replied, "I'll have someone take you down to the barn, if that will be all right. He's probably there right now."

"To the barn then," Agent Booker ordered.

Kent asked one of the residents to escort Agent Booker to the barn and introduce him to Paul. Kent walked him to the office door and said he would see him later.

Paul was tempted to duck out of sight when he saw the suit coming across the field from the lodge. He'd already been given a heads up that there was an IRS agent on the premises. As the agent approached, Paul feigned cordiality. The man introduced himself as Agent Booker with the Internal Revenue Service. "I would like to talk with you concerning your operations here," Agent Booker said. "Let's talk about your contribution. What do you receive in exchange for your work with the agricultural duties?"

"I don't get anything in exchange," Paul stated.

"Come on. You must receive cooking services, lodging, and the like," Agent Booker interjected.

"Everyone receives those benefits. It's a part of living here. Agent Booker, let me ask you something," Paul continued.

"All right," Agent Booker said.

"Agent Booker, are you married?" Paul asked.

"Yes," Agent Booker answered.

Paul then asked, "Who does most of the cooking at your house?"

"My wife does. Where are you going with this?"

"What does she receive from you in exchange for her cooking services? Do you pay her?" Paul asked.

Agent Booker had had enough. "Don't be ridiculous," he firmly ordered.

"I don't think it's any more ridiculous than your asking about what I receive in exchange for the work I do here," Paul said.

Agent Booker replied, "It certainly is. There are a lot of people living here. It doesn't compare at all to a family situation."

"I submit that it does," Paul said. "Let's say that grown children move back to a farm and live with their parents and they all work together to survive."

"That's still not the same," Agent Booker stated.

"Not the same, but the same principal. Is there a law about how many people can live together and help each other to survive?" Paul asked.

"Of course not," Agent Booker replied.

Paul then lectured Agent Booker, "Right. It's a practical matter. We've all agreed to live here, at least for the time being, and survive with what we believe is a nice standard of living. It's different than we experienced before coming here. We don't carry a wallet, don't need a watch, don't exchange money or keep a tally of what one person owes another. We're all in this together."

Agent Booker then replied, "That sounds very Utopian, but I have a hard time believing that this community is as you and Kent describe. It appears that one motivation may be to hide income, to conceal bartering of services, and to defraud the government of the taxes that it is entitled to."

That was it. Paul had had enough. "Let me be frank with you, Agent Booker. I spent most of my adult life serving my country as a soldier in the United States Army. I did so based on values that I held dear: life, liberty, and the pursuit of happiness. The country that I served no longer exists. Oh, there's still a United States of America, but not one that resembles the one I swore an oath to protect. I receive a pension for my service, and even though I don't believe I should be required to, I pay taxes on it. However, I don't intend to work where I will earn another cent that can be taxed and used to forward the objectives of those that have hijacked my country."

"Those are some pretty harsh words," Agent Booker said in a huff.

Paul was bringing this discussion to a prompt close. "I'm just telling you how I feel. You can question everyone here, but I think that you're going to find most everyone is sick of what's going on in Washington, and that's why we're here. We're here to protect ourselves and live the best way we know how as free as we can be from the intrusions of a government that preys on its citizenry."

"I guess we're through here then. I'll go on back up to the lodge." Agent Booker realized any further discussions with Paul would be futile.

Paul sarcastically replied, "Anything more you'd like to discuss, just let me know."

After completing the interviews he wanted to conduct, Agent Booker went back to town for the night. The next morning, he returned to go over the financial records. He was directed to John's office, where everything was laid out. John went about his business as Agent Booker reviewed the records. Agent Booker would ask a question occasionally and then return to his on-site inspection.

It wasn't long until Kent received notice that there was another person at the front gate wishing to speak with him. This time, Kent asked that the visitor be brought to his office.

A few minutes later, there was a knock on the door. Kent looked up and saw a man standing in the doorway.

"I'm Sheriff Baylor with the county sheriff's office."

"Sheriff Baylor, how can I help you?" Kent asked.

Sheriff Baylor answered, "This is not the type of matter I normally handle, but I've been asked to follow up on a complaint about there being illegal weapons and ammunition here. I don't have a warrant, so you don't have to cooperate at this point. I just think it would be simplest if you let me see what weapons you all have and I'll be on my way."

"All right. Follow me. I'll take you to the weapons storage area." As they began walking, Kent kept speaking. "Everything is kept in the weapons storage area except for a couple of shot guns and a twenty-two-caliber rifle. One shotgun is kept at the gristmill and the other two weapons are over at the barn."

It didn't take long until they were approaching the cavern behind the lodge.

"This serves as our primary storage facility. We use industrial dehumidifiers to keep the humidity down as best we can in areas where metal and perishable items are kept, as well as for cooling the lodge. I'll have my brother Cal show you around. He's a lot more familiar with the storage area than I am," Kent said.

Cal walked over to them as they had approached the cavern entrance.

"Cal, this is Sheriff Baylor," Kent said. "He's received a complaint about there being illegal weapons and ammunition here. I'd like you to show him what we have. I told Sheriff Baylor that you'd do a better job of showing him around since you're more familiar with where everything is. I'll be in my office when you finish."

Sheriff Baylor entered the storage area with Cal and said, "Sorry for the inconvenience, but I have to follow up on a complaint. I've been getting a few more complaints lately about a wide variety of allegations. I thought I would come over here and try to put this one to bed."

Cal said, "No problem. This is a collection of the weapons that our residents brought with them when they all came. There are three—"

"Kent told me about those," Sheriff Baylor informed Cal.

Cal continued. "Okay. We, as a community, made the decision that there would be no handguns on the premises. What you see here are a collection of pellet guns used for target shooting, a few small-caliber rifles, and several higher-caliber rifles."

"Do you mind if I take a closer look?" Sheriff Baylor asked. He had always been a gun enthusiast.

"Help yourself," Cal said.

Sheriff Baylor touched each weapon one by one and then commented, "This is a beauty. I had one of these old Winchesters when I was a boy. Do you mind if I pick it up."

Cal answered, "That would be Paul's. He's retired army and owns several of the rifles you see here. I'm sure he wouldn't mind."

Sheriff Baylor admired the rifle and then gingerly placed it back in its slot. "This is a nice collection." Sheriff Baylor looked over into the next caged security area. "That must be the ammunition."

"That's right," Cal answered.

"That's a lot of ammunition. Are you folks expecting a war?" Sheriff Baylor asked.

Cal chuckled. "We sure hope not. We just think that there's the possibility that, in the future, ammunition will become much more highly regulated or unavailable due to governmental actions."

Sheriff Baylor agreed. "I've got the same concerns. The country's changing."

"That's right. That's why we're here," Cal replied.

Sheriff Baylor said, "I'd heard about this place, but never

really could get a straight story on what you people are all about. The stories range from communists, to a paramilitary compound, or even a group of religious zealots. So tell me, why are all of you really here?"

Cal gave Sheriff Baylor a condensed version of the events and efforts that had brought the residents of Haven to this point in time.

Sheriff Baylor liked what he had heard. He told Cal, "I wish you folks great success in your endeavors here. I'll report back that I found nothing out of the ordinary or suspicious."

Cal walked Sheriff Baylor back to Kent's office. Kent then thanked the sheriff for his time and invited him to join them for lunch. On their way to the dining room, Kent stopped by and asked Agent Booker and John to join them. Kent thought that lunch with Sheriff Baylor and Agent Booker at the same table would be interesting. It was obvious that the sheriff was supportive of their community and could be a positive and perhaps even an intimidating influence toward Agent Booker.

Throughout the meal, Agent Booker had been unusually quiet, in stark contrast to Sheriff Baylor, who seemed to take pleasure in the company. The sheriff enjoyed his lunch in the dining room and asked for the check.

"There's no charge. Look around the room. None of the people you see here will receive a bill for their meal. I'd be surprised if any of them have any money on them. To the best of my knowledge, everyone in the room, except for the two of you or course, has spent some time in the garden making this food possible. It's a community effort."

"No. I insist," Sheriff Baylor said.

Kent replied, "Sorry, Sheriff. We don't use money on the premises now that the bed and breakfast business has been suspended."

"That's mighty generous of you. I guess if I had time, I'd

stay and go work in the garden for a while to earn my meal." Sheriff Baylor had sounded sincere in his comments.

Being satisfied at what he had found, Sheriff Baylor told them he was sorry for taking up their time and appreciated their hospitality. He then went out on the porch with Kent where they talked for a few minutes.

John asked Agent Booker, "How was your meal?"

Agent Booker replied, "Fine. Thank you. I've got just a bit more work to do before I return to my office and prepare my report."

"Let's go then," John said.

JM was approaching the barn at a quick pace along with one of the farmhands. Paul knew that something wasn't right and ran out to meet them. JM spoke. "I don't know if it's anything or not, but I saw a couple of people up on the ridge beyond the mill. We came back right away. I'm sure they're still up there."

JM got off his mule and pointed at the ridge. "They're right up there. I saw the sun glittering off something. I think they're looking at us through binoculars."

Paul called out to the farmhand, "Go let Kent know what you saw and ask him for three people with loaded deer rifles to go with me and check this out."

"I'll go too," JM said.

Paul looked over at JM. "I'd rather you stay here and tend to the animals and start the afternoon feeding. You don't need to exert yourself going up on that ridge."

"You're probably right," JM responded.

Paul added, "You know that Hazel would have a fit if you went. Anyway, let's get the horses saddled up so that we can be ready when help arrives."

They worked with a sense of urgency, making the preparations. When the farmhand had reached the lodge he found Kent speaking with Sheriff Baylor on the front porch of the lodge. When the sheriff heard what was going on he said that he would join them.

It wasn't long until help came trotting across the field from the lodge, bearing rifles and a look of concern on their faces. Once the sheriff had been given the horse that was the easiest to handle Paul and two others mounted up.

To reach the ridge line and meet up with the people there, Paul had to lead their group in a direction that seemed a little out of the way. There were some cut back trails that wound their way to the top. They took it slow in consideration of the animals and for their own safety.

Paul instructed the others, "Once we reach the top, I'd like you guys to hang back slightly and let me approach whoever's up there alone. It'll be less threatening than to have all of us ride up on them together."

"Paul, if you don't mind, how about I take the lead when we reach the top," Sheriff Baylor said. "There should be little confusion seeing a county sheriff approaching."

"Okay, when we get to the top, Sheriff Baylor will take the lead," Paul agreed.

Agent Booker stood up, walked over toward John's desk, and asked, "Are there any other records?"

"That's everything," John answered.

Agent Booker commented, "I haven't seen anything regarding the purchase and ownership of the land and records concerning construction of any of the buildings."

"The records I have are for the bed and breakfast business and for the operations of the community of Haven," John responded.

Agent Booker persisted, "I know that there are two corporations involved. I'd like to see the records for the ownership of the real property."

"Oh, I can't help you with that," John answered. "You'll have to get the information from Kent on whom to contact. We don't handle those records here. Kent's mom and dad put the real property in a trust account."

"Why wouldn't you have them all here?" Agent Booker asked.

John responded, "For one, there's the potential conflict of interest. And second, it's not a matter that has any direct bearing on our activities here. I thought it best for the owners to have a disinterested party responsible. Kent can give you the banker's name and contact information."

"Then I'm finished with my review here," Agent Booker said.

"Would you like me to take you back to Kent's office then?" John asked.

"Yes, I would."

John led him down the hall, gave a light tap on Kent's door that was standing open, and walked in with Agent Booker in tow.

Kent stood, smiled politely, and addressed Agent Booker. "How's it coming along?"

Agent Booker stated, "I'm through here for now. However, I do need the contact information on the person who takes care of the corporation involving the ownership of the real property here."

Kent slid open the top middle desk drawer and took out a business card. He then wrote the information on a slip of paper and handed it to Agent Booker. "Here you go. Did you find everything you need?"

"That will be all for now," Agent Booker answered. "My review here is complete. I will make arrangements with your banker to inspect those records. If there is anything further that I'll need after that, I'll contact you."

"Please do," Kent said halfheartedly.

Agent Booker informed Kent, "I'll then be submitting my report. Sometime after that, you should be contacted by my office concerning the findings with regard to the complaint that I have been investigating."

"Would you like me to walk you out?" Kent asked.

Agent Booker replied, "That won't be necessary. I know the way. I've taken up enough of your time already."

That's right. You have, Kent thought to himself. "All right then," Kent said. He bid Agent Booker farewell and, as far as Kent was concerned, good riddance.

Agent Booker walked out of the office and headed toward the parking lot.

Kent turned to John, who had been quietly observing the discussion. "Anything I need to know about?"

John answered, "No. He sat at the desk and appeared to go through everything, making a note once in awhile. Really, I don't know what he was expecting to find. From his demeanor, it would seem he was hoping to find evidence to support the allegation. I hope we've seen the last of Agent Booker and his kind."

"Me too," Kent agreed,

Once they reached the top it didn't take long to find the two people that JM had seen from below. From their dress, they appeared to be some kind of government employees. The two on the ridge heard one or more people riding up. One of them folded up what looked like a map that they had been examining when Sheriff Baylor first spotted them. They walked over to meet Sheriff Baylor as he approached.

One of the two said, "We're surprised to see anyone up here. This is normally a pretty remote spot."

"I'm surprised to see you two up here as well. One of the residents of Haven saw you from down below, and we came up to investigate. There are three other people with me just a few yards back. Who are you, and why are you up here?" Sheriff Baylor asked.

"We're county rangers with the division of forest resources. We periodically come this way and check the health of the forest. Today, we're following up on insect and disease control. We've been closely monitoring the health of the trees here. See those trees?" He pointed beyond the ridgeline. "They're some of the ones we're concerned about."

"JM saw people looking from the ridge down into the valley where they live using what looked like binoculars. You can understand their concern."

One of the rangers replied, "We just thought while we were up here we'd take advantage of the view and see if we could spot any other problem areas. We didn't mean to cause any concern."

By this time Paul had ridden up close enough to hear the conversation. Paul said, "This ridge line is within our property line. We didn't expect anyone to be up here."

The ranger said, "We're sorry if we caused any undue concern. I guess it would have been best if we had contacted you about coming on the property. However, it's just a couple of hundred yards from where our survey took us, and we didn't see any harm in walking over for a look. I hope that's all right."

Paul said, "Okay. I'll let our folks know that everything is okay. I'm sure you can understand our heightened sense of security with what's been going on around here and around the country lately."

The ranger said, "It makes perfect sense to me. I'd take precautions too."

"All right then. You all have a nice day. We'll be heading back now," Sheriff Baylor said. Sheriff Baylor then turned his horse, rode back to the others, and explained what he and Paul had learned.

Before making the slow descent back down the steep hill, Paul brought his horse to a stop and gazed into the valley below. The others did the same. "This sure is a beautiful place," Sheriff Baylor said.

CHAPTER FIVE

It was a beautiful day that Sunday. There was a great sense of anticipation, especially among the most recent arrivals. Special activities had been planned to celebrate the official establishment of the community of Haven. Following breakfast, the day began with worship services. Ted Rogers was the pastor at the church the Davidson family regularly attended. However, the number of people in Haven had grown so much, the residents thought it would be convenient if they had worship services in Haven instead of crowding into the church in town. Pastor Rogers had willingly agreed to come to Haven and preach the word each Sunday after the service in town had concluded. Everyone had taken to calling Pastor Ted "Preacher." He didn't seem to mind.

Services always began later than the people were used to since Preacher had to do the service in town first. However, the folks in Haven thought that they got the best end of the deal because Preacher usually brought his wife and stayed for the afternoon activities, which were growing in popularity. No one seemed to mind that their service started later than normal since this gave them a good excuse to sleep in and get a late start on the day. By Sunday, everyone could use a good rest.

Preacher knew this was to be a special day but didn't cut his message short. He could see the younger people squirming in their seats in anticipation of the day's events. As soon as the service finished, everyone exited the lodge faster than normal. They all headed for the grounds that had been prepared for the festivities. Tables had been moved out into the open by the nearby pond, and several activities had been set up there. The merriment began with everyone enjoying fried chicken and potato salad, followed up with watermelon. Paul still hadn't quite gotten used to providing chickens for eating. He and Sarah had always felt so partial to their birds at home. Theirs were pets. He still protected his personal birds from the pot. JM was a big help with regard to the chickens. He was more pragmatic about the whole chicken for food process. It would have been embarrassing for Paul if anyone had made an issue out of his attitude toward the birds, given his Special Forces background. Yes, he had killed and eaten one in the Special Forces qualification course, but he didn't enjoy the experience. Thank goodness for JM.

Kent put his supervisory responsibilities aside for the day as best he could so that he and Barb could enjoy the celebration. The food had been prepared the day before so that everyone would be able to attend and enjoy the planned activities.

Much to her chagrin, Kent's sister-in-law, Jean, had been pushed into acting as the spokesperson. Her husband, Cal, had been very supportive and had taken a leading role in setting things up, but it was Jean who people wanted to act as the day's spokesperson. She had earned a lot of respect from the residents by the calm manner in which she handled the everyday matters at the lodge and was always available to anyone needing a kind word or a problem addressed. Barb's sister, Sally, had volunteered to help set up age appropriate games for the children. Together they had put together a lot of activities for the residents of Haven. All of the preparations for the activities were now complete and ready for the community to enjoy.

As things were starting, it didn't take long for the first disruption to take place. A couple of the more mischievous dogs had found their way to the fried chicken. The chicken had to have a guard put on it while someone restrained the dogs. Cal hollered at a couple of the young men to grab the dogs by the collar, take them over to the barn, and pen them up. First problem solved.

To begin the official celebration of their new life in Haven, Jean asked Kent to say a few words. Kent had become the unofficial mayor of the community. As he approached the makeshift podium, there was an exaggerated applause from those assembled. Kent raised both hands up high, signaling for the group to be quiet. Then he made some opening comments.

Kent spoke distinctly and seriously. "Good afternoon. Welcome to the inaugural celebration of our new community. Welcome to a life as free from the intrusions of government as we can make it. Our country is no longer what we once knew. Here in Haven, we have intentionally created a community that upholds the ideals our country once knew; a community we pray is pleasing to God. I thank you for all of your effort in making this community a reality, a place I hope you consider a dream come true. Have a great day."

Applause followed as Kent stepped away and Jean came back to the podium.

"I hope everyone enjoyed their lunch," Jean said. There was some more applause. "Now, we've got a lot of activities planned for this afternoon, and several will be going on at the same time. You can go from activity to activity as you wish.

In this area, there will be games and activities for the younger children, led by Sally. There will be target shooting over at the range and swimming and canoe races at the larger pond. Fishing will be available at the farther pond. Then there's horseshoes. Finally, there will be volleyball and softball if there are enough people who want to participate in those activities. Later in the afternoon, there will be a scavenger hunt. The bell will ring fifteen minutes before the scavenger hunt so that anyone wanting to participate can finish up the activities they're doing and come back here for instructions. Any questions?" She paused for a moment and said, "Then let the activities begin." Everyone stood up and began moving to the activities they wanted to participate in.

John had gone back to his office to check on an administrative matter and heard the phone ring. It was one of the guards down at the front gate. The guard said there was a family asking for help. He was hoping Kent was available. John wasn't sure where Kent was, but as he was walking out of the lodge, he came across Cal. "Cal, one of the guards called and has asked that someone come and help him. There's a family at the front gate asking for help."

"Did he say what kind of help?" Cal asked.

"No. He just said that they were asking for help," John answered.

"Okay. I'll go and see what they need." Cal walked down to the front gate.

JM was on his way over to the range and saw two of the younger men, teenagers actually, off by themselves. JM walked over and asked, "Are you fellas going over to the range?"

One said no and the other shook his head.

"So what are you guys doing this afternoon?" JM asked.

"We're just hangin' out," the first answered.

"Yeah. Just hangin' out," the other echoed.

JM then asked, "Don't you want to participate in some of the activities that have been planned for this afternoon?"

"No. They're stupid," the first one said.

The other crossed his arms and gave the silent treatment.

"What do you mean stupid?" JM asked.

"It's kid's stuff."

"What would you rather be doing?" JM was concerned about their attitude.

"Going to the mall and hanging out with friends."

"Obviously, there's no mall around here. And you know that the mall near us hasn't opened back up, even if you were in town," JM pointed out.

"So how would you know that? We never go anywhere."

JM replied, "Believe it. I know they're closed. One of my responsibilities is to know where things can be purchased. Anyway, it's safe here. We don't have to worry about all of the troubles going on outside our community."

"I can take care of myself," the boy replied.

"I'm sure you can, but you're here now. You might as well make the best of it," JM said.

"We'll just hang out here."

JM made a suggestion, something the boys might enjoy. "I'm headed over to the range. Come on over if you'd like to try it out."

"Yeah right," one of the boys said sarcastically.

The other boy continued the silent treatment.

JM knew the boy's parents by sight and thought he'd better discuss the conversation with Kent later.

Cal saw one of the guards standing by the family that needed help as he approached. He asked, "What seems to be the problem?"

The guard answered, "This is the Hendrix family. They've fallen on hard times and heard about Haven."

"That's right," Mr. Hendrix stated. He walked away from his car and family before he spoke again.

Cal followed him.

"I'm a carpenter. There's no work. I can't pay my rent, and we've been evicted. I can't buy groceries to feed my family. My wife is pregnant, and we can't get any medical care. I heard about you all up here and thought I'd come and see if you would help us."

"How much money do you need?" Cal asked.

Mr. Hendrix replied, "It's not money so much. We need a place to stay, and we need some food. Our kids haven't had a good meal in a week."

Cal looked over at the kids, who appeared to be around five and seven years old. His wife appeared to be well along with her pregnancy. "So what do you propose?"

Mr. Hendrix spoke firmly. "I'll provide all the carpentry work you need if you'll just help us out however you can."

"How about we go up to the lodge for now?" Cal suggested. "We'll park your car in the lot until we get your family and things unloaded."

"Anything you say. Thanks. God bless you," Mr. Hendrix said gratefully.

"All right. Would it be okay if I ride back up to the lodge with you?" Cal asked.

"Sure. Hop in."

Mr. Hendrix introduced Cal to his family. They drove up and stopped in the parking lot in front of the lodge.

"Leave your things here for now. I know what you'd like to do first." Cal led them over to the tables and offered them some of the leftover chicken, potato salad, and watermelon. You'd think they had been offered the finest dining in a fancy restaurant. The kids enthusiastically dug in.

"While you finish up here, I'll go and look for Kent. I'll be back in a few minutes."

JM arrived to find Paul leading the marksmanship activities. "Paul, I thought I'd practice up on my shooting skills. It's been awhile."

Paul said, "That's what the range is here for. Let's see what you can do."

While they were getting things situated, JM asked, "Paul, did you see two young men on your way over here this afternoon?"

"Yes. They were off by themselves. I didn't really think much of it."

JM said, "Well, I walked over to them and discovered that they are quite unhappy with their life here in Haven. They miss the life they had before coming."

Paul replied, "I'm sure the same can be said for some of the adults too, don't you think?"

"Of course," JM said, "but from my perspective, it's kind of like a bunch of people surviving in a life raft, reminiscing about how good things were on the ship before it went down. Instead of being thankful that they're still alive and have a safe place to be, they're complaining about what they no longer can have."

"That's human nature? We all have a tendency to look back with rose-colored glasses."

"I guess you're right, Paul, but I don't think it's healthy to dwell on the past like they're doing."

"From their perspective, they aren't dwelling on the past. Their view is that they're looking to the future. You know as well as I do that once things straighten up outside of our community, some of our residents will leave. That doesn't mean that they're necessarily unhappy here. It's just that their view of an ideal life on this earth consists of things that can't be offered here in Haven."

JM said, "I see what you mean. I'd planned on mentioning the discussion that I had with the boys to Kent. I'm just worried that they could get in trouble given their current way of thinking."

Paul replied, "It wouldn't hurt for Kent to discuss the boys' attitudes with their parents to bring it to their attention. However, my guess is that they already know and are dealing with it the best they can."

After they finished discussing the boys, JM started his target practice.

Cal saw Kent over by the canoes and went over to talk with him. He explained the situation with the Hendrix family and asked how Kent wanted the matter with them handled. Kent suggested that Cal and Jean might want to put them up at the end of the second bunkhouse. Kent thought there was still room there. He then asked Cal to bring Mr. Hendrix to his office in the morning. He'd need to complete an information form, consent to search form, and security background check form. In the meantime he asked Cal to introduce them to some of the residents and ask them to make themselves at home. Kent said he was sure there was nothing to worry about, but he'd like Cal to make sure someone discreetly kept an eye on them until they could be checked out.

"I'll take care of it," Cal said. He walked back over to the tables where the Hendrix family was seated and told them that they could go ahead and enjoy the activities. It was a special day in Haven and they wouldn't want to miss it. At the end of the scheduled activities, he'd meet back up with them and show them where they'd be staying.

Cal introduced them to some of the residents that were nearby and then left them to enjoy the rest of the afternoon. He spotted one of the farmhands and caught up with him. He gave the farmhand a condensed version of the Hendrix family's story and said that Kent would like someone to discreetly keep an eye on them for now. He agreed to do so.

JM had finished up his target practice but had stayed at the range to help Paul as others came to participate. It was probably about two thirds into the time allocated for the planned activities when JM noticed several of the men walking toward the lodge. JM asked Paul if it would be all right if he went to see what was going on. That was fine. JM hurried up to the lodge and found several of the older men gathered in the reception area, trying to get reception on the television.

JM asked, "What's going on?"

"I think we're at war," one of them said.

"I know we're at war, at war with the Islamic terrorists," JM replied.

Another said, "No, not that. It sounds like we've been attacked again. One of the kids was listening to the radio and heard a bulletin and then everything went dead."

"That's all you've heard?" JM asked.

"So far," the first man answered.

JM said, "Let's find Cal and ask him to turn on his shortwave radio and see if we can find out exactly what's going on."

One of the men nearby said, "I saw him just a few minutes ago. I'll go and see if he can come." It wasn't more than a couple of minutes when the man returned with Cal.

"What's going on?" Cal asked.

One of the other men answered, "The boys were listening to the radio when a bulletin came on saying there had been a terrorist attack in our country, and then the radio went dead."

"Let's crank up the shortwave radio and take a listen to what's going on," Cal said. He had become a ham radio operator when he was in the Boy Scouts many years ago. He had been fascinated about being able to communicate with only dots and dashes. That led to his lifelong enjoyment of the radio set he owned.

Everyone present followed Cal through the lodge, out the back door, and into the cavern where the shortwave radio was set up. The antenna was farther up the mountain, so that the reception would be good. The radio was alive with news on many frequencies. It didn't take long for Cal to tune into one with something pertinent.

"Reports of violence in the streets have been coming in from across the nation, following news of a bombing at a mall outside of Atlanta, one in Indianapolis, and another in Boise..." The report then described how Islamic U.S. citizens were being attacked and general disorder had erupted in most of the country's major cities.

Cal left the radio set on the frequency that was broadcasting up-to-date news and walked over to Kent as he entered the storage area. Cal quickly told Kent what was going on.

Kent replied, "Our country has been a powder keg ever since the government started their rapid march toward socialism, and the country has never come back since the run on the banks. Sure, some of the banks are back in business on a limited basis, but many of the small, local banks have yet to reopen, and people are desperate to get their money out. It's not surprising that the Islamic terrorists would take advantage of the unrest our country is already experiencing by adding additional fear into the mix through their violent acts."

Cal said, "I know. But certainly this will impact us here in Haven."

Kent replied, "I'm sure it will. I just don't know how or to what extent. I think it would be a good idea to have a community meeting to discuss the unrest in the country and what it might mean for us here in Haven."

Cal responded, "Yeah. We need to get this out in the open and have an idea of what we'll do."

Kent said, "How about you ask Jean to make an announcement concerning the meeting at the end of today's activities. We'll put it on the announcement board too."

As the activities were winding down, Cal walked over to the Hendrix family and offered to show them to their quarters. He said the accommodations weren't spacious but that the common areas made up for a lot. He walked them around the lodge, showing them the meeting area and the dining area. He also showed them Kent's office, where Mr. Hendrix would need to go first thing after breakfast the next day. Cal then took them to their room in the bunkhouse. The Hendrix family was obviously grateful for the room and board. Cal said that he hoped they'd be comfortable and looked forward to seeing them the next day.

Jean called everyone together that hadn't gone up to the lodge to learn more about the recent events in the country. "I hope everyone has had fun today," she said. She had the organizers stand for a round of applause. Then all of the winners of the various competitions were recognized for their achievements. She then announced the community meeting that would be held at 10:00 a.m. in the dining room the next morning and the topic of discussion. Also, due to all that was going on, she informed them that the scavenger hunt was going to be rescheduled for another weekend. Jean let everyone know that sandwiches had been prepared for supper and were in the boxes on the tables. She encouraged everyone to enjoy the rest of a beautiful day.

Once Jean had finished, she walked over to a nearby table and joined some of the ladies that were visiting. "Wow! What a day," she said.

Barb responded, "I think it went great, except for several of the guys leaving the activities to listen to the news. There was the news that came over the radio. That was bad enough. But none of us can stop worrying about Kent's mother. He's taken his dad to the hospital everyday to check up on her. There's not been any improvement, bless her heart. I go with them when I can get away."

"Cal's been the same way," Jean replied. "He's felt guilty about not getting up there every day with Kent and his father. This is tearing them all up." After a short pause she said, "I'm sorry, enough of that, let's talk about the fun we had today." Jean then looked over to Paul's wife, "Sarah, you looked like you were having a good time.

Sarah really had enjoyed herself. It had been a long time since she had paddled a canoe. "It was a great day, and I'm glad that I didn't have to patch anyone up. Normally, at least one person will need medical care on a day like this with all that went on."

"I'm glad you could come and join us for a while today," Jean said. "It was nice to see you out on the lake having fun."

Sarah stood up. "Thanks. I will see you at the meeting tomorrow."

"See you tomorrow then," Jean echoed, as did the others.

"Sally, you did a nice job with the children's activities today. The kids really had a good time," Jean said.

"Thanks, Jean. You all gave me a lot of ideas," Sally answered. "I've always enjoyed working with children. It was nice to see the new kids have a good time too. They seemed pretty uneasy at first, but they came around quickly once they got involved. I think the water balloon toss was one of the favorite activities."

John's wife had been unable to step away during the afternoon and find out what was going on up at the lodge. She asked, "So, what have you heard from the guys? What's going on?"

Jean replied, "Cal came down and told me that they'd heard on the news that there had been at least three presumed terrorist attacks across the country and that there have been riots in some of the major cities."

"I guess it was only a matter of time," Barb said. "That's why we're here, isn't it?"

Jean thought about Barb's comment. She paused a moment and then replied, "That's what originally put things into motion, but I would want to be here even if there was no threat to our country. I like it here. I like that our community is based on shared values."

Barb agreed. "You're right. I didn't mean to imply otherwise. I like it here too. However, I believe that Kent would still be doing contracting work at Fort Bragg had it not been for the recent actions of our country's leadership." Barb then looked at her sister. "Sally, you've been here a little while now. How do you like living in Haven?"

Sally answered, "I had some misgivings when you first described the plan to me. But as I took time to think about what it all meant, the idea grew on me. I think it was hard to consider the transition I was going to make when I left teaching in the public schools. Once I made the decision to go ahead and retire, the decision to come here came easy, and I've never regretted it. It's been very meaningful working with the kids in a home school environment. I'm seeing progress every day."

Barb replied, "I'm glad you're here. It just wouldn't be the same without you. Jean, how do you feel about things here now? You've seen a lot, and I'm sure you know a lot more about the inner workings of our community."

Jean looked at peace as she answered, "I think it's been a good change for Cal and me. Even though we're both busy here, we see a lot more of each other and share almost every meal together. That was rare before. I never really thought about what a chore shopping was and keeping up with a budget. Life is a lot simpler here. I don't worry about finances anymore and certainly don't miss making trips to the store."

"You're right, Jean." Barb had focused so much on what she had that she hadn't really thought much about what she had left behind. "I don't miss shopping trips either. And I spend a lot more time with Kent than I did before. I know Kent would have liked to continue working in the construction business at Fort Bragg for a while longer, but I think if he were to honestly answer you he'd say he likes most things about Haven. I know that he likes being so close to his family, especially now with his mother in the hospital with her health failing. I think the thing he would say he misses most is getting together with his old friends from high school. They'd get together every month. Whether it's worth the tradeoff for him or not, I don't know. I hope so. Other than the worries he has about his mother, Kent seems happy enough."

Jean agreed, "Yes. Cal enjoys being here with family too. He owned and operated the feed store most of his adult life. This has probably been the biggest adjustment for him to make since arriving in Haven. I do think he's adjusting well though."

Barb then asked John's wife, "How are you and John enjoying being a part of Haven?"

She replied cheerfully, "Oh, we both love it. John has taken up well with most everyone here, and he enjoys working so closely with Kent and Cal. It's working out great."

The ladies talked a while longer before calling it a day.

After the guys stopped listening to the information coming across the radio, Cal lingered in the storage area, thinking about what it all meant. He had been hesitant to give up the feed store and come to Haven but was quickly realizing that life as he had known it had been on the brink of ending before they had ever talked about the idea of setting up a community to escape to. It was like the bow had been drawn and the arrow released. It just hadn't struck yet. It was only a matter of time until life in the United States would be unalterably changed into the image of the long-time enemies of democracy and capitalism. He didn't know why it had taken so long to see it. His wife certainly had. Cal had been steadfastly clinging to the idea that things would return to normal as they always had in the past. He figured that that must have been how many of the people in Europe had felt when Adolf Hitler began garnering power in Germany. They just couldn't accept that life would be unalterably changed until it was too late. Now the time had come for the United States to experience the rapid reshaping of the country into a socialistic entity that continued to eat away at the fabric of what had once been the United States of America. Anyway, his parents needed him. It wasn't until Kent spoke to him that he awoke from his own thoughts.

"Cal, you look zoned out. Is something bothering you?" his brother asked.

"I guess it should, but it doesn't. I believe it's just sunk in what we're about here in Haven, why we really created this oasis in the middle of a country gone astray. It's like we're a remnant that so often is mentioned in the Old Testament of what once had been the norm in our country."

Kent said, "That's some pretty heavy thinking. I thought maybe you were worried about what we heard on the radio."

"Sure. That is distressing. It's a shame that such evil exists in the world, evil that would kill innocent people," Cal said.

Kent replied, "No one's innocent in their minds. I assume it's either Islamic terrorists or Islamic terrorist sympathizers. It makes about as much sense as when they brought down the World Trade Center Twin Towers and attacked the Pentagon."

Cal stated, "That means that no one is safe, especially now that the leadership in Congress seems sympathetic to those who wish to do harm to our nation. If they weren't, why would they even think about letting any of the prisoners at the detention facility at Guantanamo Bay free in our country and provide them benefits to boot?"

"Yeah. It's crazy," Kent agreed. "It's hard to understand how the citizens in our country keep going along with the harebrained proposals coming out of the White House and Congress. It's like Europe on the eve of World War II. They were blind to what was going on then too."

Cal replied, "Yes. That's exactly what I was thinking. So, what do you think we're going to discuss at the meeting tomorrow?"

Kent answered, "I'm not sure, but we don't have long to wait and find out. Hey, I know it's getting late, but I haven't been up to see Mom all day, and I know Dad would like to go. You want to join us?"

"Yes, I really would," Cal said. "I'll see if Jean wants to come, and we'll meet you all out in front of the lodge."

"Okay," Kent said. "I'll go and get Dad and be back in a few minutes. I'll see if Barb wants to go too. See you soon."

CHAPTER SIX

It wasn't a typical Monday morning. The cook and his kitchen crew for the day had prepared their usual breakfast, but the main topic of discussion was the news that had been heard the previous night about the bombings and rioting taking place across the country. It seemed so far away now since they had escaped to Haven. It was their refuge from the realities being faced by so much of the country. Despite the troubling news, the Hendrix family was thankful to be eating breakfast together as a family again. They had often gone with little or no food so that their kids wouldn't suffer. Whether or not this current place of safety would last or not, they didn't know. But they were thankful for the day. As soon as they had finished breakfast, Mr. Hendrix went to Kent's office. No one was in, so he sat in a chair outside his office and waited for him to arrive. A few minutes later, Kent walked over and said, "I hope I haven't kept you long."

Mr. Hendrix said, "No. I just sat down."

Kent said, "I was talking with John about the meeting we're going to have later this morning. Come on into my office." They entered. "Go ahead and make yourself comfortable." Kent motioned toward the chairs in front of his desk. As Kent held out some papers he said, "If you would, please fill out these for you and your family. We require these from everyone that resides here in Haven. There's the information form. We use it to help in determining what work activities to suggest. It basically reveals your knowledge, skills, and abilities. Next, there's a request for certified criminal record search. And finally there's the consent to search form. We reserve the right to inspect anyone's property as a matter of safety to the person and for the safety of others. After we finish here, you'll need to go see my brother Cal. He'll tell you about how to get things you might need. He'll also make available to you a place to store any valuables you'd like to secure during your stay. He'll provide an itemized inventory of the items you leave and give you a copy. Oh … Here's a copy of our policies and procedures that we recently put together. Any questions?"

"Why the criminal record check?" Mr. Hendrix asked.

Kent answered, "We do all we can to make Haven a safe place for all of our residents. From time to time, someone comes to the community that no one knows, such as you and your family. Since no one can vouch for you personally, it's a way we have to at least do some cursory screening."

"I see. That won't be a problem," Mr. Hendrix replied.

"If there are no other questions, I'll leave you here to complete the paperwork. You can leave them on my desk and then go over to see Cal in the storage area. I've got a few more preparations to make before the meeting. I hope you understand."

Mr. Hendrix responded, "Certainly. Thank you for accepting us into the community. I know you won't regret it."

"It's nice to have you. See you at the meeting." Kent walked out the door, leaving Mr. Hendrix alone in his office. Kent wanted to speak with JM before the meeting.

JM walked over to the barn when he saw Kent approach. "How'd it go with the new arrivals?"

"Pretty routine. John will run the criminal record search through Sheriff Baylor's office. He'll get it to the Clerk of the Superior Court for processing. It turned out to be a real blessing when the sheriff showed up that day. He's been very helpful. So, what did you want to see me about?" Kent asked.

JM explained, "As I was going to the range yesterday afternoon, I saw the Rivera's boy and his friend and spoke with them briefly. I asked them why they weren't participating in any of the events. They said they thought they were stupid."

"Sounds pretty normal for boys their age," Kent noted. "That's just a rebellious time of life. I'm sure you remember."

JM remembered. He was glad he didn't have to deal with what these boys were going through. "Yes. I'm just concerned that they're going to cause trouble for others."

"So, what do you think would help?" Kent asked.

JM responded, "They stated a strong desire to go to the mall. That's the way they described it, the mall of all things."

Kent said, "Okay. I think we can arrange that. They'll be pretty disappointed showing up at the mall to find it closed for business. I'll talk to the boys' parents and see what they would think about an outing. The boys will still be rebellious, but they probably won't be asking to go to the mall again anytime soon."

JM replied, "I didn't think about you giving them their way, but it will be kind of funny if their parents go along with the plan. I imagine they've had to listen to the boys complaining for a while."

"JM, we need to leave for the meeting pretty soon, any last minute suggestions?" Kent asked. Kent was a little apprehensive about how a discussion of terrorist attacks would be received.

"No. I just think we need a frank and open discussion about the possibilities."

"Okay. See you there soon." Kent then headed back to the lodge.

Everyone was assembled except for those guarding the front gate. While approaching the podium, Kent looked across the faces of the residents of the community. Many had looks of apprehension. There was a hush as he stopped and began to speak.

"Before we begin with today's business, I'd like us to have a moment of silence for those that lost their lives around the country in the attacks and in the violence yesterday." With all that had taken place across the country, Kent felt led to open the meeting with a word of prayer. After the moment of silence and prayer, Kent resumed the meeting. "I'd like to thank everyone who made yesterday so special: those who prepared the food, planned and led the activities, and everyone else involved. Yesterday was a great day for Haven. However, with that great day came news that was disturbing. It was disturbing in that people across our country have been killed and injured as the result of presumed terrorist activities. Many now live in a heightened state of anxiety, which seems to have been with us since our government started taking over and running private industry. The fear goes beyond that of concern for the fabric of our country but for physical well being as well. I'm sure you recall that it was in anticipation of events such as this that we conceived the idea of creating this community, a safe haven from the disasters that we anticipated would soon strike our country and our home. Now, so that we can minimize our concern about these events, I thought it would be beneficial to discuss, as a community, how these events might affect us and what we should do in anticipation of or in reaction to them."

Few serious issues came up as the meeting progressed. Some were concerned that phone lines had become more unreliable. Others were upset that radio and television transmissions were being affected by the economic crisis the nation was facing. The last topic was one that got everyone's interest.

Kent asked, "Now what do we do when people show up at the front gate needing help. Fortunately, we do have some surplus food that we are harvesting at this point and we are able to provide some assistance. You've all met Mr. and Mrs. Hendrix and their boys." Kent nodded to the Hendrix family. "They recently joined our community and are already proving to be a real asset. We still have what you could call vacancies. However, our space is not unlimited, nor is our food. The question is, how do we handle people who arrive when space and food is no longer available?"

One comment came from the back. "Just don't let 'em in."

Kent replied, "How about if they're hungry? Do we feed them first, or do we send them away hungry? Or if they're hurt and need medical attention, do we help them first and then send them on their way? It's not as simple as it appears on the surface. We think of ourselves as God-fearing people. For example, in the New Testament, in James 2:16, it says, 'And one of you say unto them, depart in peace, be ye warmed and filled; notwithstanding ye give them not those things which are needful to the body; what doth it profit?' I don't see how we can, in good conscious, send people away hungry. Let's do some brainstorming on this dilemma and see what we can come up with. Any ideas?"

Paul had been thinking about this problem for quite some time. While serving in the Special Forces, he had been involved in developing security for their unit while assisting indigenous populations with humanitarian aid. Now, he was hoping the day wouldn't come to Haven when this hard decision would have to be faced, but it looked like they were closing in on it. Paul raised his hand.

"Go ahead, Paul," Kent said.

"From a security standpoint, we need to fortify the front gate. First, we need to make Haven inaccessible to vehicular traffic. I would suggest we dig a sizeable ditch across the entry area outside our main gate from hill to hill, so that it can't be bypassed. This could be accomplished with the backhoe in a few hours. We could have emergency bridging material on hand that could quickly be moved into place to accommodate a vehicle. Then we would need to have at least three people on duty at all times. From a humanitarian viewpoint, I would suggest we construct a shelter that people could stay in overnight, say if a family arrives at the end of the day. Instead of sending them away after dark, we could offer them food and shelter for the night before sending them on their way in the morning."

"Thanks, Paul. Those are good ideas. Does anyone have any comments concerning Paul's suggestions?" Kent asked.

One person asked, "When do you think we need to dig the ditch?"

Kent answered, "I don't think it's time yet. I think we would want to do so once we are at capacity. Any other ideas?"

Cal asked, "What if they say they don't have anywhere to go or they need money to get where they might be going? Maybe we need to establish a benevolence fund. Most of us meet together each Sunday. We study God's Word and worship him. We're called upon to tithe, and even though we don't use money here we still have a responsibility to have an offering for God. Perhaps helping others would be a way of fulfilling that obligation to some extent. This situation makes me think of the story of the Good Samaritan. The Samaritan was a good neighbor, so should we be. Even if we're not able to provide for all of the needs of everyone that shows up at Haven's doorstep, I believe we have an obligation to do something."

"Point well taken," Kent said. "Cal has made an important

observation concerning this matter. By a show of hands, I'd like to get an idea of how many of you are able and would be willing to contribute money to a benevolence fund to help people in need."

There were a large number of hands raised around the room.

"Thank you. All of you that raised your hands, I would appreciate it if each of you would stop by John's office and make arrangements to contribute toward a fund to help passersby in need. John, you'll need to build up a supply of cash since checks and credit cards are no longer accepted at many places. Barb, do you think you could help John get cash from the bank in town?"

"I think so," Barb answered. "I've developed some contacts that are friendly to what we are doing here in Haven. We still have some great friends at the church in town also."

"Okay. Any other ideas?" Kent asked.

One of the younger men asked with a smirk on his face, "What do we do if someone or a group of people refuse to leave? Can we shoot them?"

"I think Sheriff Baylor wouldn't take kindly to us murdering people," Kent said.

Paul spoke up. "That does bring up a good point. Soon we will need to develop some comprehensive rules of engagement. We need specific procedures on determining how needs we learn about are to be met and when use of force would be deemed appropriate. I think it would be good to ask Sheriff Baylor to review what we come up with so that he knows exactly what our plans are and the justification."

Kent asked, "Paul, I know you're busy with JM farming, but I'd like to once again take advantage of your military experience with regards to security. Would you be willing to meet with the guys that have been performing guard duty and work up a draft? We can then post it on the bulletin board for everyone to read and make any comments or suggestions before presenting it to Sheriff Baylor for any suggestions that he may have on the subject."

"Sure. I don't think it will take long," Paul answered. "I've got some pretty specific ideas on what it should include already and would look forward to working up a proposal with the others. A lot of it has already been developed in the security implementation plan that JM and I previously developed that included practice drills. We'll start with that."

"Thanks, Paul. After you all work up the revised plan and we get it approved here, we'll run it by Sheriff Baylor for his comments and work on conducting the security drills that you and JM developed. We'll want most everyone to participate in them. I guess the next thing to do will be to shift assignments around so that we can put more people at the gate at any one time. Does anyone else have anything more they would like to discuss before we adjourn this meeting?" Kent paused and looked around the room. "There being no more discussion, then we will adjourn for now."

Kent saw one of the parents of one of the boys that JM had been concerned about on his way to the range. He walked over and said, "I've been planning on talking with you about your son."

The father asked, "Did he get into some trouble?"

"No, nothing like that. JM just happened to bump into him yesterday. JM said your son seemed unhappy here. I know that the teenage years aren't ever easy, but I just thought I should ask you about it."

"Yes. He and his friend would rather be at our old home, which is no longer an option. We were in the process of losing our house when we moved here. I'd been laid off, along with a lot of other people where I worked, due to the downturn in the economy. We just couldn't keep up with the bills and the mortgage payment any longer."

"Yes, you and a lot of other people too."

"That's right. Our son is just not taking it well. He can't understand all of the changes that are happening in our lives. He resents being picked up and moved."

"That's pretty typical. I was wondering if there's anything we could do to help," Kent asked.

"If you have any ideas, I'd sure like to know. We're at our wits end with him. He's a good boy. He's just unsettled right now."

"JM thought that an outing for him and his friend might help."

"What kind of outing? We don't have outings anymore."

"How about a trip to the closest mall?" Kent suggested with a smile on his face.

"The last I heard is that it's closed and has been closed for some time."

"Yes, it is. I imagine you've told your son that too?"

"Yes we have. He doesn't believe us."

"Then maybe a trip to the mall might be enlightening," Kent said. "We could set it up for you to take him and his friend to two or three malls so that they can both see for themselves that none of them are open. That won't make them happy, but at least they'll understand that things have changed in the world."

"That just might help. I agree. It still won't make them happy, but it'll give them something to think about."

"Then if you'll see Cal he can get you directions to the nearest malls and provide you a vehicle if you don't have one. You can plan on that tomorrow if you would like."

"We'll tell our son tonight and talk about this with his friend's parents so that he and his friend can both go. They might as well both get the benefit of the outing."

"It's settled then. I hope things improve with your boy. Good luck tomorrow." Kent then went back to his office for a few minutes before going to lunch.

After lunch Kent went over to the farmhouse to get his dad. They would go to the hospital and see his mother. When they arrived at the hospital, Kent's mother still showed no signs of improvement. Kent spoke with the doctor. The doctor told Kent that it was unlikely that his mother would rebound. Kent's dad asked if they could bring her home. The doctor said they could if she had constant supervision, preferably by someone with medical training. Kent dialed the number for Haven praying that the call would go through.

"Haven, this is Jean, how may I help you," came the answer.

"Jean, this is Kent."

"Is something wrong?" Jean asked.

"Mom's the same. They don't expect her to get better. Dad asked if she could come home, and the doctor said she could if she had constant supervision, preferably by someone with medical training. Are either Paul or Sarah available?" Kent asked.

"No, but I could get them and try calling back soon," Jean offered.

"I know it's hard to tell from the work that they do in Haven, but they're both trained nurses. Would you ask them if they'd be willing to take care of Mom?" Kent asked. "I know Paul will be concerned about the garden work getting done, but I'm sure JM can take care of it with help from some of the families that have come to Haven recently."

"I'll go find them right now, and I'll either have one of them call you back or I will," Jean said.

"Thanks. I'll be looking forward to your call." Kent hung up. He and his father waited.

As Cal approached the storage area, he was surprised to see someone that appeared to be snooping around. "May I help you," Cal asked.

"Oh, I was just looking around," Mr. Rivera said. "I wanted to make sure I knew where to go if I needed anything."

"Well, this is the place," Cal said a bit irritated. "I thought you'd already seen the storage area."

"Hey, I thought it was neat how you could get information on your radio. How do you get such good reception down in this valley?" Mr. Rivera asked.

"See up there," Cal said as he pointed to a particular spot on the ridgeline.

"Yeah."

"The antenna is up there," Cal said. "That way we can always get good reception. I've even spoken to people in other countries on the radio."

"Wow, that's great," Mr. Rivera said a little overenthusiastically.

"I thought you and your family were helping the cook out today." Cal didn't like people around the storage area when he wasn't there.

"I just took a short break and wanted to stretch my legs. I'm on my way back now," Mr. Rivera said in a casual manner.

"All right, I'll see you later." Cal made a cursory visual check of the area and didn't see anything out of the ordinary. He picked up a bag of seed that JM had asked him about earlier.

―――

"This is Kent," he said as he answered the phone hoping for an answer from Haven.

"Hi Kent, its Paul. Jean told me about the situation with your mother. Yes, Sarah and I will be happy to look after her."

"Thanks, Paul. That would be great. I'll let the doctor know. I think we'll be bringing her home today."

"I do have one request to make though," Paul said.

"Anything," Kent replied thankful for the help Paul and Sarah would be giving.

"At least for the time being, I would like Sarah and I to move into the farmhouse so that we'll be near your mother all the time."

"Sure," Paul said. "That's a great idea."

"Sarah and I will work out a schedule so that one of us will be there with your folks around the clock. That way Sarah and I can continue to help JM with the gardening when were not on duty at the house."

"Thanks, Paul. I'd say go ahead and start moving in if you want. I'm thankful for you and Sarah, and I know my dad will be relieved that mom can come home."

"We'll be moved in and waiting on you all."

"Thanks, Paul. See you soon."

Kent was relieved to know that his mother would be able to come home. It didn't look like she had long to live. She had said she felt like she was smothering and could hardly take a breath. She wanted to come home.

The so-called audit that Agent Booker conducted at Haven had not turned up anything damaging to Haven's cause. In fact, Agent Booker couldn't help but be impressed with the clever manner in which the accounting had been set up. He could tell that they had gone to great lengths to have everything be above board. He had only done a little better through his spy in Haven. If he didn't report back to Senator Bates soon, he would have a lot of explaining to do. It was time. He placed the call and was put on hold by the receptionist. The background music on the phone was inspiring patriotic music. Agent Booker thought it was kind of ironic to be listening to patriotic music while waiting to talk with Bad Boy Bates.

"Alexander, I've been looking forward to hearing from you." Actually B. B. despised the weasel of a man; however, he did find him useful. B. B was gifted at finding what value a person could bring to the table and then taking full advantage of the situation.

"I've been wanting to call you, Senator, but I wanted to have something worth taking your valuable time." Agent Booker hated to kowtow to the Senator, but Senator Bates was a force to be reckoned with.

"What have you got for me," B. B. asked. "Did you find anything during your audit?"

"Not in the audit, no. Their books are squeaky clean. They're not generating any income up there that we can legitimately tax."

"Come up with something," B. B. demanded.

"Well, while I was there, I overheard that they've been giving advice to other groups that want to join together in similar living arrangements." Agent Booker knew that this wouldn't go down well with the Senator, but felt obliged to tell him.

"Great, that'll be even more people avoiding their patriotic duty," Senator Bates said in a very sarcastic manner.

"What duty would that be?" Agent Booker asked.

"Paying taxes man, are you daft?" B. B. said incredulously.

"I was sure that's what you meant, Senator. I just wanted to make sure I understood you correctly." Agent Booker realized he opened his mouth sometimes when it would be better to just keep it shut.

"We can't have people deciding that they can just pull up stakes and stop pulling their fair share. We've got to make an example of them." B. B. knew that Kent was too smart for his own good. He'd seen that in him back in high school. B. B. thought, *This can't stand.*

"I have been able to get some information that might be useful," Agent Booker offered, hoping to give the Senator something so as to leave the conversation on a good note.

"All right, I'm listening." B. B. knew that he was a patient man to put up with someone like Alexander.

"I've got a sketch from my man on the inside and where they are vulnerable. My man at the state pen has given me contact information on a person that was just paroled that could be helpful in shutting Haven down."

"Do what you have to do, but I don't need to know the details. I can't afford to be linked to any of this. And don't let anyone else know that we're in communication. You got that," B. B. demanded.

"Loud and clear boss," Agent Booker said meekly. "I just thought you'd like to know that something's being done. You said yourself that you want to make an example out of Haven. We can't have this type of living arrangement spreading around the country."

"Thanks, Alexander. Keep me informed. Just don't allow my name to be linked to any of this." B. B. knew he was going out on a limb trusting Alexander.

"Got it. I'll call when I have more." Agent Booker hung up thankful that he'd placed the call and more thankful that it was over.

CHAPTER SEVEN

When Kent pulled up to the farmhouse, Paul and Sarah were on the porch waiting on them. His brother Cal and Jean had slipped away from their normal duties so that they would also be present when they arrived. Though everyone was sad to see how Kent and Cal's mother had declined while she had been away, everyone was glad she was finally home. After getting her settled, Kent's father asked them all if he and Vera could have some quiet time together. Cal and Jean reluctantly went back to work. Kent went back up to his office to try and get caught up after being gone for so many hours. Paul and Sarah went back out on the porch.

Over the next few weeks, Paul and Sarah developed a routine that Kent's parents grew accustomed to. Kent's mother continued to complain that she was smothering. Her breathing was labored. Everyday Kent would come and spend hours at his mother's side. He'd always been a mama's boy. And if his mother had a favorite, it was Kent. Cal never resented Kent for the closeness his brother and mother had. Cal had always considered himself a daddy's boy.

Cal would find time everyday to spend with his mother as well. They were a close family. During this time in their life, they made a point of having daily family devotionals. They would normally have them at the kitchen table that sat just outside the room their parents now used as a bedroom. Kent would sit at the table. It was angled so that his mother could see him from her bed. Pappy would sit in a chair next to the bed with a Bible in his lap and follow along showing Vera the scriptures when she was able.

During these weeks John had struggled to keep up with all of the duties that Kent had performed in the past. Fortunately, one of the families that had come to stay in Haven included a man that was obviously gifted in administration. He would arrive promptly every morning and ask John what he could do to help. He explained that he had lost his mother not long ago and had some understanding about what the Davidson family was facing. He said that he thought it was his Christian duty to step in and do what he could with the talents that God had given him to lessen their load during this difficult time in their lives.

The entire community seemed somewhat subdued. They could all sense that death hung in the air. Most of the people that had come to Haven were strong in their Christian beliefs. They weren't afraid for Vera so much as they were sad for what the family was going through. They knew that when Vera did pass away that to be absent from the body is to be present with the Lord.

Kent was having trouble coping with the realization that his mother was near death. Intellectually he knew that his mother would soon be in heaven with God. She would no longer feel smothered. She would no longer have labored breathing. What Kent was having trouble with was that she would no longer be there for him to turn to, to confide in. Kent became more despondent with each passing day. He had spoken with Preacher about his anxiety and understood the scriptures that he'd been directed to. Finally, Kent was no longer able to concentrate adequately on his work.

Without John helping him, Kent wouldn't have been able to continue. Once a day Kent went to the office and met with John who gave him a quick update and gave him whatever had to be signed that day. John was glad that he could be of service to his friend in his time of need.

After completing his work in the garden one morning, Paul walked into the farmhouse. He could sense there was something wrong. He hurried to the back bedroom and saw Pappy sitting in a chair next to the bed with his body leaned over, his head beside his beloved, and his right arm across her chest in a solemn caress. Sarah was in a chair in the corner leaned over with her head in her hands. As soon as Sarah realized that Paul had entered the room, she stood up and motioned for him to follow her out of the bedroom.

"Paul, Vera has passed."

Paul reached his arm around Sarah to comfort her as he wiped the tears from his own eyes on the sleeve of his shirt. "We've been expecting this for the last few weeks," he said.

Sarah replied, "She passed quietly. Pappy was there by her side. It seemed that we could both feel the life leave her body. We've been quietly mourning for the last few minutes. I guess we need to contact the doctor from the clinic and ask him to take care of the paperwork. I think he'd be willing to come down and confirm her death. Then we could conduct a funeral and bury Vera here on the property in accordance with her wishes. That's what Pappy wants, in the old cemetery out behind the house beyond the large oak tree. They've each talked about wanting to be laid there when they are called home to be with the Lord."

"I'll go up and tell Kent and Cal that their mother has passed away. I'll pass it along to the others as well," Paul said. "I know that a lot of people have come to love her and Pappy. Even though she wasn't able to get out and mingle much, she made an impact on those around her, especially at the meal times we shared in the dining room in the lodge."

Sarah replied, "She was a special lady. I don't know how Pappy's going to get along now with Vera gone."

Paul thought it will be easier for Pappy than it would have been for Vera had Pappy passed first. "I've got the feeling that he will immerse himself in work. It probably won't be long until we find him out piddling in the garden, something to occupy his time and his mind. He knows that's what Vera would want. She wanted him to make the most of what life he has left, before he's called home and they are reunited in heaven."

Sarah looked down. "I hope you're right. They were so close. It's hard to watch this happen."

Paul comforted Sarah. "You're right. I've grown fond of them both too. I really enjoyed hearing the old stories the two of them would tell about courting, their early life, and life on this property. It was so good to hear Vera share her fond memories when she rallied shortly after returning home here. I'm just glad that you and I were able to be a part of helping make that happen for them. I know Pappy is grateful for the extra time they had to share together in their home."

"I know," Sarah replied.

The two of them stood there for a few minutes before Paul finally left to go and tell the news to Kent and Cal. Paul gave a tap on Kent's door and entered when he was motioned in. "I've got bad news. Your mother has just passed away."

Kent placed his face in his hands and began sobbing.

Paul hardly knew what to say. He stood there in silence for a moment and then said, "She passed in peace. She just slipped away while your father was holding her hands. He's sitting there with her now. Sarah's watching over them to make sure your dad's okay."

Kent abruptly stood up and hurried out the door obviously going to the farmhouse to be with his mother and father. Paul then looked for Cal and found him going through some things in the storage area and told him the same thing he had told Kent. He too left for the farmhouse.

With these notifications done, Paul walked over to John's office and told him the news. Paul then suggested to John, "I'll have someone pass the word so everyone will know that the family is grieving. I guess we'd better call the doc to take care of the formalities too."

"I'll call Preacher," John said. "He'll also want to know."

"I'll call him" Paul replied. Paul called Doc, who said he'd be right down. Then he called Preacher. Preacher said he'd be there by supper time and would visit with Mr. Davidson and find out what his wishes were concerning Vera's passing.

It didn't take long for Doc to arrive. He noticed that the gate had been reinforced and had more people manning it. He stopped and spoke with one of the guards.

"What's with the changes? You all expecting trouble?"

One guard replied, "You never know. We just want to be ready."

"Well, I'm here to see Mr. Davidson."

"Yes. We know. It's a shame, Miss Vera's passing."

"Yes, but she's been in a bad way for quite a while now."

"I know. Drive on up. They're expecting you." The guard opened the gate while Doc drove through.

Doc had been in and out of the Davidson's home many times to check on Vera during the last several weeks. It had come to feel like visiting family. Paul met him on the front porch and led him to the back. "She's in here."

Doc cleared his throat. "Mr. Davidson, I'm so sorry for your loss."

Without moving from the bedside, Pappy just nodded, acknowledging Doc's condolences.

"Mr. Davidson, I'll just be a minute. I'm required to check Mrs. Davidson's body to confirm things so that I can prepare the required paperwork."

"I understand." Pappy stood up and stepped out of the way as Doc conducted his examination.

Doc was done with his task in a moment. "I need to put a time of death on the certificate."

Sarah said, "It was about a quarter to noon."

"Thank you. Do you want to have her taken to a funeral home and prepared for visitation?"

Pappy shook his head. Paul motioned for Doc to follow him out of the room.

"Doc, Vera wanted to be buried in the family plot out in the back of the house. A couple of the boys are already working on making a casket from wood grown on the property. Also, Cal previously made arrangements for a burial vault with the funeral home in town. We're just waiting on Preacher to arrange the ceremony."

"Sounds like things are in order then. Is there anything else I can do for you all while I'm out here?"

"No. None that I can think of," Paul replied. "I really appreciate your coming out here so quickly."

"It's the least I could do. I have looked after the Davidson's medical affairs for many years. In fact, they helped me get started when I set up practice here about thirty years ago. They're great people. Vera will be missed."

"Yes, she will," Paul agreed.

"I'll be going now. If you'll again extend my sympathies to Mr. Davidson, I'll see myself out."

Paul waited about an hour before going back into the bedroom where Pappy was again leaning on the bed, caressing Vera. "Pappy, we can't leave Vera here. It's just not proper. I think it's time we moved her body until it's time for her funeral."

Pappy gave a mournful wail as he stood up. He didn't look up. He just said, "All right. It's time."

Sarah accompanied Pappy out into the living room so that he would not have to watch her body being moved. Paul stepped out onto the porch and called in the three guys he'd asked to help him when the time came. They reverently entered the bedroom. The four of them gingerly lifted Mrs. Davidson and moved her to the pickup waiting outside. They carefully laid her in the bed on the truck and drove her up behind the lodge to the entryway for the storage area. They had previously decided that the back part of the cavern would be a suitable spot for such a contingency as this, for the temporary storage of a body. The cool temperature would help in storing the body until the funeral, which would probably be in the morning after breakfast.

Preacher arrived just before supper and was waved on through the gate. He went directly up to the farmhouse, where he was expected. Paul was sitting out on the porch, waiting on him. Paul stood up and walked down the stairs and said, "Preacher, I'm glad you're here. We've moved Vera's remains up to the storage area to keep overnight. Pappy would like to have a funeral in the morning after breakfast around ten."

"Sure. Do you know what he has in mind?"

Paul replied, "Pretty much. He said that Vera had talked about having Cal's wife play the guitar and sing her favorite hymn, and she hoped you would say some words about how she's at home with Jesus and how she hopes everyone else can come and be with her at their appointed time. She wants you to tell everyone as plainly as possible how they can be saved and know that they too can have eternal life through Jesus Christ."

Preacher explained, "That's what I typically do at a funeral in some form or another. I'll take care of that. Do you know if Mr. Davidson wants the congregation in town invited to attend the funeral?"

"I know he wouldn't mind, but he wouldn't want anybody to feel obligated to come if they don't want to. Are there any from town that you think would want to come?" Paul asked.

"Yes. There are several couples in the congregation who knew the Davidsons well and thought highly of them. If you want, I'll contact them and let them know about Mrs. Davidson's passing and the funeral arrangements so they can come if they are able."

"That sounds good, Preacher."

"I guess I ought to go on in and pay my respects to Mr. Davidson."

"He's sitting in the living room," Paul said. "He's been sitting there since the boys took Vera's body out. Even though he knew this was coming, he's taking it hard. It's easy to understand though. They've spent most of their lives here together. It's like a big piece of him is gone."

After Preacher gave his condolences to Mr. Davidson, Paul said it was time to head over to the lodge for supper. Pappy declined. He said he'd like everyone else to go on over but that he'd prefer to have some time to himself. They could bring him back a cold plate if they wanted when they had finished. Normally, Paul and Sarah walk over to the lodge, but Preacher was going to drive over so he could leave directly from there when he was ready to go. They all rode over together, agreeing that Pappy deserved some quiet time alone to mourn Vera's passing.

Kent knew that he should call his brother Brad in DC before joining the others in the dining room. Brad had not been very close to the family in recent years, but he deserved to know that his mother had died. Kent dialed Brad's cell phone number.

The voice came on the line, "Brad."

"Brad, this is Kent."

"Hi, Kent. It's been a long time. How are things going?" Brad asked.

"Mom passed away," Kent said choking back the tears. It was difficult for Kent to keep from breaking down as he had said those words. There was no reply. "Brad, did you hear? I said Mom died."

"Yeah, I heard. I had to think about what you said for a minute. How's Dad taking it?' Brad asked.

"Like you'd expect," Kent said. "He's not coming to supper. He needs some alone time."

"Had she been ill?" Brad asked.

"She took a fall down the stairs awhile back and never fully recovered," Kent said. The doctor thought she was going to be okay, but she never snapped back. She developed congestive heart failure and has been doing poorly ever since."

"Why wasn't I told about this?" Brad asked.

"Would it have mattered?" Kent replied. "Would you have come?" There was long pause on the phone. "If you're coming for the funeral, we'll delay it. Otherwise we're going to have it in the morning in the family cemetery out behind their house."

"Go ahead as scheduled," Brad said. "I can't get away now. Tell Dad how sorry I am and that I wish I could come and be there with you all."

"Okay," Kent replied.

"Kent, there was something else I'd been meaning to talk with you about."

"What's that?"

"You know Senator Bates," Brad said in a matter of fact tone.

"You know B. B. and I went to the same high school and entered the army at the same time."

"Yeah, I knew that," Brad said. "Well, I've not been privy to the discussions he has with the inner circle but I overheard bits and pieces that made me think about you."

"How's that?" Kent asked. His interest was piqued.

"Well, I've heard that he's in fairly regular contact with somebody in the IRS somewhere in North Carolina."

"We were audited recently," Kent said. "We're waiting to hear something back."

"Well, there has also been talk that the Senator is not happy with communists. I did some checking around, and what he's really talking about is self-sustaining communities like you all have in Haven now."

"Why would he have a problem with that?" Kent asked.

"It seems there are a couple of issues he has. First, he thinks it's unpatriotic to withdraw from society and live independently. And second, he's concerned about the loss in taxable revenue. It's like the people that become a part of a community like Haven fall off the grid as far as taxes goes."

"It can't really make a noticeable dent in the overall revenue can it, Brad?" Kent asked.

"With just one place, no. But there are other communities being founded using the same principles that you have there."

"We have had some people stop by now and then to ask how we structured things here," Kent replied. "I don't see a problem with giving some informal advice."

"I don't know this for sure or not, but I think Senator Bates holds you personally responsible and wants to put a stop to people establishing and running self-sustained communities."

"What can he do about it?" Kent asked.

"I don't know, but he's well connected in places that you'd

never imagine," Brad said, "My advice is simple: watch your back. Oh, and please don't mention this part of our conversation to anybody. I know that the Senator wouldn't take kindly to my speculating about his business, especially with you."

"Then why does he keep you around, knowing you're my brother?" Kent asked.

"I think it might have something to do with what Sun-Tzu said, 'Keep your friends close, and your enemies closer.' I don't really think he considers me his enemy, but I'm starting to think he's placed you in that category. If so, then he might think my relationship with you might be beneficial to him in the future somehow. I don't know."

"Thanks for the advice, Brad. I've got to get to the dining room. Preacher will be saying some words about Mom's passing."

"Kent, I'm sorry about not being there more. Give my best to Dad. Bye."

"Bye, Brad." Kent said. Kent thought that Brad's mood seemed different than usual. He thought perhaps it had something to do with their mother's death. He wondered if the audit in some way had anything to do with B. B. *Time to join the others*, he thought.

When he entered the dining room, there was a somber feeling in the air. Vera wasn't well-known personally by some of the newer residents, but everyone knew of the contribution that she and Pappy had made in making their community possible. The ones that did know her were saddened by her death. Once it seemed that everyone who was coming to supper was present, Kent asked Preacher if he would go ahead and say a few words. Preacher agreed.

Preacher rose and said, "I'm sure you all know that Mrs. Davidson passed away a little before noon today. Any of you who would like to pay your last respects can do so in the morning after breakfast. Mr. Davidson has asked that a graveside service be held at about ten in the morning. Anyone who would like to attend is invited to do so. The service will be at the Davidson family cemetery a short ways behind their home. I hope to see you there in the morning." He then sat back down. After visiting a short while longer, he said that he needed to get back to town and notify a few people about the funeral arrangements.

After Preacher had left, Sarah fixed a plate for Pappy. Then Paul and Sarah walked back to the house to find Pappy still sitting in the living room as they had left him. Sarah offered him the food, which he declined. She then insisted that it would be best if he would come into the kitchen, sit down, and eat something. He reluctantly complied. After Pappy had finished eating, they all went to bed early.

Preacher returned the next morning with six members of his in-town congregation who were able to attend Vera's funeral. They were joined by most of the residents of Haven. After everyone was assembled, Kent and Cal led their father to the family cemetery for the service. Seating had been provided for Mr. Davidson, his sons, and daughters-in-law. The others stood in a small semicircle just behind them. As requested, Preacher presented a stirring message, making clear that the only way to heaven was through the sacrificial death of Jesus Christ, that he had died on the cross for the sins of the world and that salvation was only possible by accepting him as Lord and Savior. Cal's wife stood up, moved over, picked up her guitar, and sang Vera's favorite song, "Victory in Jesus."

After the service, Kent and Cal led their father back to the house. The others returned to their normal duties. While walking back to the lodge, John and Paul caught up with Kent. Paul said, "JM and I are ready with a draft security implementation plan whenever you'd like to see it. We've been putting this off for quite awhile in consideration of your family's situation, but we need to get the plan reviewed, approved and implemented."

"I know you're right, but I can't deal with it right now. How about getting together with the others and plan the implementation? I've got to go and be with my family."

Then John spoke. "I'm sorry to have to bother you with this at this time. But we've continued to receive more families. We've nearly reached capacity. We need to do something soon."

"You've got my approval," Kent said. "Thanks, John. And thanks for everything you've been doing. I couldn't get through this without you and your help. You're a great friend. And Paul, thank you for all that you and Sarah have done for us."

"It's been our pleasure," Paul answered, "But I want you to know I've had plenty of help from the others."

"That's right," John agreed. "Everyone has chipped in to keep things going."

Kent had not recovered enough following his mother's death to resume his work, so Cal took charge of the security plan. After lunch, Paul and JM met him at the front gate. Paul had left Sarah to look after Pappy. Paul knew that his experience in Special Forces would give him a different perspective on what security measures would be appropriate given this situation. Paul handed Cal a copy of the plan that he and JM had prepared.

"JM and I worked this up using the initial security implementation plan that we developed previously as a starting point. There's an important difference in the guidance we received and what we came up with on this one though."

"That's right, Cal," JM said. "We just couldn't come up with a portable bridge that could easily be put in place and taken down. We'd envisioned something like a drawbridge, but it just was too much."

"It wasn't practical," Paul said, "so we came up with an alternative plan. We propose digging a ditch from hill to hill, leaving a narrow portion of the road intact. We've discussed this portion of the plan before. The ditch will provide a barricade from unwanted visitors, except in one narrow spot. On the far side, we would place posts in the road so that you could only approach the entryway at a slow rate of speed. That way the guards couldn't be surprised by a fast-moving vehicle. A slower-moving vehicle wouldn't have as much energy to push through. JM, show Cal where you had suggested the poles be placed."

They walked to the other side of the entry gate. JM placed six X's in the dirt with the heel of his boot to indicate where each pole would be positioned. "Here, here, here, here, here, and here. We set up small, temporary posts to test where the best locations would be. This is what we came up with so that trucks could still get by, but only by driving slowly."

Cal asked, "If a large truck was coming down the road fast, wouldn't it be able to knock the posts down and keep on coming?"

"What we've got in mind is really more than a post," JM replied. "It's really a segment of a larger tree. The posts will actually look like stumps. No, a truck wouldn't be able to push through."

Paul then walked over to Cal. "I also wanted to discuss this with you. Look at the diagram on the next to the last page. This is how we recommend that we position everyone around the property in the event that we actually come under attack. The rally point would be the storage area, where the weapons and ammunition are stored. We would then disburse to the areas indicated, which would provide an overall perimeter."

"JM, tell Cal about the last page."

"Okay." JM walked over to Cal and they both looked at

the last page together. "We set up the following schedule for a practice drill. Zero hours means the time we start the drill. At zero hours, the alarm is sounded. Zero plus ten would be ten minutes into the exercise. The time goes from there. At first, we'll need to walk through it a few times. After that, we can try it out as if it were an actual alarm. The times shown that Paul and I came up with are our best guess as to what it would take to get everyone armed and into position. With a little practice, we think we could be in position within ten minutes of the alarm sounding."

"Okay. I'll read through the whole plan in detail and let you know if I have any questions. Otherwise, I'll have Kent take a look at it and then give our residents a day to look it over and make any comments they have before faxing it to Sheriff Baylor for review. I appreciate the comprehensive job you guys did in putting this together."

Paul said, "I thought the portable bridge would be doable, but JM came up with the zigzag approach. I think this method is better. It's the same approach the military uses at checkpoints in high danger areas. The benefit is that it gives us a way to enter and exit the property more quickly during an emergency. In the event of an attack, the narrow entryway could be blown with prepositioned explosives, which will then block all vehicular entry."

"Thanks. I'll see you guys later."

Kent finally got to where he wanted to check on what was going on. He knew that he would grieve for his mother for a long time. He knew she was heaven, but he felt lost without her here. When he arrived at the lodge, Kent immediately went to his office and saw some papers on his desk. He read through the details of the security plan that he knew his brother had been working on with Paul and JM. It looked good, so he made a copy and took it to Jean for posting. Kent wanted to get this to Sheriff Baylor right away and then get on with the practice exercises that were mentioned once he had a reply and they were ready to go final with the plan. Kent hoped that the plan would never have to be executed in earnest, but things were looking worse and worse around the country. It seemed that the remote area Haven was located in had created a geographical barrier, which bought them time. It made it harder for anyone with ill intent to reach them.

Kent had received reports from time to time from Cal. He had been in contact with some ham radio operators where he had moved from. Things were getting bad. Burglaries and murders were way up. Many people had become a law unto themselves as local law enforcement was incapable of maintaining law and order as the economic fabric of the country disintegrated. Some people became lawless in desperation to meet the basic needs of themselves and their families. Those who were lawless to begin with became emboldened to even greater atrocities than they had previously committed. Kent stopped by Cal's office to visit for a few minutes. Frankly, he needed a break from the stress that came with his responsibilities in Haven. "Cal, how are things going for you?"

"All things considered, I'd say they're going all right," Cal said. "John was able to get phone service today and take care of most of the high-priority business transactions for everybody which have been in limbo for the last few days."

"I'm glad to hear that," Kent said.

"What did you think of the security plan?" Cal asked.

"The plan that you, Paul, and JM came up with looks good."

"Great." Cal paused for a moment and could see the strain in his brother's face.

"Bro, how's it going for you?"

"Okay. Things are plugging along well," Kent replied.

"No. I mean, really. How are you?" He emphasized the *you*.

"I guess I'm just a little tired. It's been one thing after another for so long. It never seems to settle down."

"I know what you mean. Do you ever regret getting involved, in coming here?" Cal asked.

"Certainly not," Kent said. "I'd hate to think what it would be like if we hadn't. Unlike most of the people we used to live near, we live in the relative safety of Haven, in stark contrast to what they're facing. And even though I know we're making preparations for intruders, I feel safe here anyway."

"I do too. You know what?" Cal asked his brother.

"What?" Kent replied

"I've noticed some other benefits that I would have never thought about before coming here."

"Like what?" Kent asked.

"Well, have you noticed that most of the people who moved here who were overweight have lost a lot of that excess weight and are looking more fit?" Cal pointed out.

"I'd never thought about it, but you're right, Cal. I guess with all of the physical work that we all share in and the good and healthy meals provided by the cooks, it's not surprising that the health of our community has improved."

"And for another," Cal continued, "I think most of the families now get to spend a lot more time together. Before, everyone was too busy to spend much time with each other. And even though we're busy here, it's busy in a different way. You know, we all do something all the time, even if it's just sitting and reading a book. What our work consists of now is contributing to the effort of providing food and a nice place to live, as opposed to making a boss happy. Before coming here, we worked for money so that we could afford to do what we wanted to do. Now we don't work for the money. We get what we need by producing it ourselves."

"That's right," Kent said. "I like not having to carry a wallet. I've even stopped wearing a watch most of the time. I just seem to know when it's time to eat; and if I don't remember, I can hear the bell ring from most anywhere on the property. I like not having to consider the tax ramifications of business transactions. You know, I could go on and on about what I like concerning our new life here. Thanks for bringing it up."

"So, Kent, is there anything you miss from your old life?"

"Before I arrived here, I thought that there would be a lot that I would miss. However, I've been so busy with things here that I haven't really had time to think about it. So I guess the bottom line on answering your question is that there's nothing in particular that I miss. As long as I'm here with Barb, you, and Jean, and Dad, here could be about anywhere. Is there anything you miss?"

"Kent, I'm with you on this one. It was a blessing for Jean and me to come here when we did. I've spent a lot of quality time with Mom and Dad. We would have missed out on that. Yes, I'm glad we came too."

No suggestions came in concerning the security plan, so Kent asked John to fax it to Sheriff Baylor. He made sure that John had read the final version of it first. John then faxed it to the sheriff, who quickly responded that it looked good and just not to kill anybody if it could be helped.

Having the sheriff's okay, Kent asked Paul and JM to get the planned barricades installed, the ditch dug, and everybody that performed guard duty up to speed on the plan and what would be done given the different possibilities.

All of the residents of Haven were assembled and received a briefing on the plan and given the training schedule. It took two weeks of practice before the residents were confident that they knew what to do in case they heard the real alarm. Practice drills were conducted periodically, but the practice alarm had a distinctively different sound than the actual alarm would have. Kent hoped that the community was ready in the event that the security plan had to be implemented in earnest.

CHAPTER EIGHT

The last couple of months had become fairly routine. The fall harvest was complete and the food safely stored away in the bowels of the cavern, where the cool air would keep them fresh until next year's crops came in. A lot of effort had gone into putting in place the security plan that had been developed. John Turner's wife had trained the dogs that she had brought to Haven with her. She had a passion for animals as a child. The hours that John had spent working at his law practice had given her time to get heavily involved with dog training. She didn't mind that John had become so involved helping Cal run the place for Kent. In fact, she admired him for it and didn't resent the hours he spent on those duties. She had used her time training her dogs for their new environment. The dogs had been trained to alert their handlers when an intruder was identified. She had also trained the people that were to be posted at strategic positions how to keep the dogs near them, along with some basic dog handling skills. The residents had mastered the security drills they had been conducting, which made most everyone calmer despite the hardships being endured by the general population of the country.

From coast to coast, there continued to be isolated terrorist attacks that created fear and anxiety, mostly in the more populated areas. However, equally devastating had been the results of the government's quest for taking control of the major components of the country's economy. This had global consequences. Most major business transactions were more and more influenced by political factors rather than free trade among nations. Efficiencies of production were replaced with incompetent management created by Congress with the consent of the president. Then, when the troubles became public, Congress would hold hearings and blame the people who had reluctantly enacted the inept policies created by those conducting the inquisition. It seemed that most of the people bought the farce, and those who verbally acknowledged the reality of what was going on were labeled out of touch and solely motivated by an unpatriotic political agenda. You were either lockstep with the government or you were considered out of step with the will of the people. This was largely aided by the dumbing down and outright misrepresentation of what was going on by the mainstream media. If Kent and the others had not isolated themselves in this self-sustained, remote community, they would have each been considered out of touch and a potential security risk.

At midmorning, the relative calm of the community suddenly came to an end. Kent received a call on the field phone that a few large vehicles had pulled up and stopped short of the barricade that had been constructed. He was told that several armed men in camouflage uniforms stood beside their vehicles. One had held up a bullhorn and said, "Send out your leader within thirty minutes." He was told that they looked like they might be National Guard.

Kent sounded the alarm, and the community quickly assembled in their prepared positions throughout the property. The front gate area was well covered, as it was the easiest point of access to Haven. Kent then asked John to immediately contact Sheriff Baylor or anyone from his office and let them know what was going on. Kent then hurried over to where Paul was and asked him to accompany him to the front gate to confront their antagonists. Kent respected Paul as a military man and thought that his presence would help guide him in quickly making the right decision. Paul readily agreed, and they promptly hurried down to the gate with Paul's dog, Lady.

As they approached the gate, tension was heavy in the air. They immediately heard instructions given through the bullhorn. "Come on over. We need to discuss your situation."

Paul turned his head toward Kent and said in almost a whisper, "Let's ask them to meet us halfway."

Kent nodded. When they came up even with the gate, Paul said in a loud and firm voice, "We'll meet you in the middle." Kent could see a couple of the men across the way talking with each other. A moment later Kent heard, "Okay, step out in the middle. Don't bring that dog." Paul took Lady over to one of the guards and told her to sit and stay. Kent and Paul then complied with the instructions and walked to the middle. As they were walking, the two men that had been conversing walked out to meet them, their weapons resting in their arms.

As they met, Kent was the first to speak. "Now that we're here, what is it that you want?"

"Your property has been condemned. You will all have to evacuate. We are here to help your community relocate."

Kent replied, "What do you mean condemned?"

"You know, the government is confiscating your land. You have to get out."

Paul instinctively knew that this whole situation was a setup. These were not military personnel. These were a bunch of thugs. Paul said, "Then we need to get our attorney to come and talk with you. We'll be back in a few minutes with him."

"No. That's not how we're going to do this. One of you will stay with us while the other goes for your attorney."

"Kent, you go. I'll wait here and talk with these soldiers about the situation until you come back."

"I don't like this," Kent responded.

"Go ahead. I'll be here."

"Are you sure?" Kent asked.

"Yes. Go now," Paul said with emphasis. Paul knew that they weren't going to let both of them walk safely away. They needed a hostage. With Kent out of the way, he could make a move, try something. Otherwise they were both goners.

"Okay. I'll be right back with John. It won't take more than five minutes. I'll be right back." It was clear that Kent was rattled. Kent still hadn't returned to 100 percent following the death of his mother. He hurried off to get John.

Paul knew that he had less than five minutes to resolve this situation one way or the other. If Kent returned with John and they came out here, the three of them would be in harm's way. He said, "I'll be waiting here."

As soon as Kent was out of sight, the thugs led Paul to a position by one of their vehicles. Paul squarely faced the one that appeared to be the leader and said accusingly, "I know you're not military."

"How do you figure that?"

"Easy. None of you have any military bearing. You look like a bunch of bullies trying to get your way by force. What do you really hope to accomplish here?" Paul asked.

"We're tired of struggling for every meal for us and our families. We've decided that we're through struggling. We heard about your community up here, and we decided that we want what you have and we're going to take it."

"Now how do you plan to do that?" Paul knew this was going to turn out bad.

"Can't you see that we are strong? We can take your sissy bunch of people just like that," he said as he snapped the fingers on his right hand.

"Tough guys, huh? You haven't really thought this through, have you?" Paul realized there was no easy way out. These guys meant business.

"How do you figure?"

"Don't you expect that our community will have some firepower to meet yours?" Paul asked even though he didn't expect this line of questioning to accomplish anything. He had to try.

"You may have some weapons, but word on the street is that you're a bunch of Jesus freaks, turn the other cheek and all that."

"You want some food. I'm sure I can convince the community to give you some food." Paul knew he had to be decisive and quick; otherwise Kent and John would be walking into a trap.

"We're not going to take a handout. We're going to take it all."

"I'd suggest you all turn your vehicles around and leave. At this point, we will call it no harm no foul." Just as quickly as he had made the statement and caught his captors by surprise, Paul pivoted and briskly walked back toward the gate. As they turned to grab him, he lengthened his stride.

The thug yelled, "Stop or I'll shoot."

It seemed as if the world had gone into slow motion as Paul considered the words that he had just heard. He thought about Sarah and the love he had for her. He thought about the salvation that he knew he had through Jesus Christ's sacrificial death on the cross. He thought about the Bible, in the book of Romans 5:7, where it said, "For scarcely for a righteous man will one die: yet peradventure for a good man some would even dare to die." In that moment, Paul was at peace with his decision to continue moving toward the gate, knowing that death was a very real possibility. He thought about what a great life he had been given the opportunity to live. He heard a gunshot.

The residents near the front gate had been watching in fear as Paul talked with the men out front. They were relieved when they saw him turn to walk back to the gate. The relief was short-lived when they heard the voice over the bullhorn. They were horrified when they saw one of the men raise his rifle, aim at Paul's back, and pull the trigger. A shot rang out, and Paul's body dropped to the ground. Paul's dog, Lady, pulled away from the guard and ran over to where Paul's body lay. The dog whimpered and lay with his head facing Paul's chest. The gunshot was immediately answered with the distinctive sound of a fifty-caliber machine gun. The gun let off a few rounds, spraying dirt up in front of the man who had shot Paul. No one was hit, but it sent the thugs scurrying behind the safety of their vehicles.

Throughout the community of Haven, everyone had heard the sound of the gunshot ring out, echoing throughout the valley. That was immediately followed by the distinctive sound of machine-gun fire. Even those that had never heard the sound of a machine gun in person recognized the distinctive rat-tat-tat the gun barked out. Most of the residents lifted a silent prayer to God on behalf of their fellow community members. Mr. Rivera was especially startled. *Has anyone been killed?* he wondered. *What will happen next?*

Kent and Cal hadn't been informed of the complete plan that JM and Paul had developed. They had left JM out of the security force using the premise of JM's age. They had also failed to include the information about the machine gun, which Paul had a license to own but had not secured in the storage area. Paul had been concerned that the knowledge of there being a machine gun on the property would have been disturbing to some of the residents. Paul and JM had discussed the best placement for the weapon and had prepositioned it at the site, along with the ammunition, in a concealed position. It was highly unlikely that anyone would have ever stumbled across it where it was located. The only other person that knew about the weapon was the farmhand that fed the ammo through when JM practiced with the weapon. Along with JM, the farmhand was assigned to the position where the gun was located.

Paul had taken the time to train JM and the farmhand on the use of the weapon. They had packed it out on JM's mule away from the property and practiced a few times until they were comfortable with its use. Paul had assigned JM to fire the weapon and the farmhand, knowing that the young man might have a tendency to shoot too soon, to feed the ammunition. JM had the maturity needed to make the decision on if and when to fire. Age had taken the edge off. The farmhand had thought JM was too old, but he quickly learned at their practice sessions that farming had kept JM physically and mentally tough.

JM desperately wanted to shoot the men responsible for Paul's apparent death, but Paul had told him to shoot to kill only as a last resort. All he had done was lightly pull the trigger, letting off a few rounds, aiming for the area immediately in front of the men and their vehicles. Paul had taught him to hold fire after the initial burst. His position would probably have not been discovered, and he and the farmhand could remain where they were for future developments. Against his instincts, JM followed the instructions Paul had given. He and the farmhand stayed concealed in their positions.

The would-be intruders were taken aback by the distinctive sound of the machine gun fire. "We'd better get out of here, Beast," one of the intruders called out to their leader.

"So much for turn the other cheek Jesus freaks," he replied.

A couple of the other guys were scanning what they called the compound with binoculars. They were trying to determine where the machine gun fire had come from and try to size up what the people on the other side of the gate were planning. One saw a guard with a camera that obviously had a telescopic lens. He was taking pictures in their direction.

The man standing next to the one who had shot Paul said to the other, "Why did you have to do that? We're really in trouble now."

Beast spoke harshly, "You saw what he did. He just walked away and refused to follow instructions. I had no choice."

"You did have a choice. You made the wrong one. Now were murderers."

"Not if no one knows," Beast said with an evil crazed look on his face.

"How do you intend on making sure no one knows? Can't you see that they've taken pictures of us?"

Beast said bluntly, "We'll have to kill the witnesses and get the camera."

"How do you propose to do that?"

Beast explained, "We'll hold tight until after dark. Then we'll make our move. Hey you," Beast said as he pointed to one of the guys off to the side, "take a couple of guys back toward the main road and set up a road block. Make sure that no one comes through. We don't need any interruptions here. Got it?"

The other guy with a voice that sounded rather put out said, "Yeah. I got it."

JM and the farmhand stayed in their concealed position. They could see that one of the guards was making a call on the phone. They had no way of knowing that they were unable to reach anyone. They needed to let the others know what had happened, but they wanted to talk to Kent.

Two of the guards tried to talk the other out of what he was planning to do, but he couldn't be persuaded. He was going to rush over to Paul and pull him by the arms to the safety of the shelter. Not realizing he was dead, they were hoping to get him immediate medical attention. The guard crouched low, hurried over to Paul, and dragged his lifeless body to the safety the shelter could provide. Thank goodness it had been made to withstand gunfire. Lady followed close to Paul's body. They were hoping that Paul had only been injured, but their worst fears were quickly realized when they confirmed that Paul was dead. They decided that one of them needed to let the others know what had happened. One of the guards volunteered and rushed away toward the lodge, the shelter screening his movement. They were thankful that there was no reaction from the enemy.

As quickly as he could, the guard hurried toward the lodge and met Kent and John, who were hurrying down the hill toward the front gate. "Kent! John! Paul's been shot! He's dead. They shot him in the back as he was walking back to the gate."

Kent had suspected that the guys at the front gate weren't legitimate, but he had been persuaded by Paul to go and get John. It was obvious that Paul's real intent had been to get him to safety, away from trouble. Paul had sacrificed himself for him and the others. He would have to personally tell Sarah, but that would have to wait for now.

"It sounded like machine gun fire. Did they hit anyone else?" Kent asked.

"No. They only fired one shot," The guard answered. "The machine gun fire apparently came from our side."

"We don't have any machine guns," Kent stated. "I've seen the whole arsenal."

John interrupted. "Apparently you haven't seen everything."

"I guess not." Kent paused and looked at the guard and then at John.

"I wasn't able to reach Sheriff Baylor or anyone else for that matter," John said. "The phone lines are dead. Also, Cal hasn't been able to call out on the radio either. It appears that someone has disabled the antenna. The only option we have to communicate with the outside is to get someone up on that ridge with a cell phone and try to call Sheriff Baylor or someone else for help."

The guard had another idea. "If we're unable to make a call, then maybe we should send someone on horseback to ride out of here for help."

"That's a good idea too," Kent said. "John, would you find JM and talk to him about who would be best to ride up to the ridge to try making a cell call, and if that proves unsuccessful to ride out for help?"

"Sure. Where would he be?" John asked.

"I don't know. He's not assigned a specific position. Try to find him and meet me back in my office as soon as you can. I've got to go talk to Sarah. I want to have her hear about Paul from me. I'm the one that asked him to accompany me, and it was for me and the rest of us that Paul sacrificed his life. Oh," Kent said, almost with the sound of panic in his voice, "and tell the others as you are looking for JM what has happened and to stay alert."

"I'm on it," John replied with a sense of urgency.

Kent then looked over at the guard, "You can go ahead and get back to the gate and help the others. Tell them if there's any movement on the other side of the barrier toward the crossing to blow it before they get there." Kent was glad knowing that the explosives were already in place.

"Will do." The guard hurried back toward the front gate.

John took a copy of the security plan to help guide his way and went from position to position, looking for JM. As he approached the farmhand he saw him and JM manning a machine gun. They were situated in a well-concealed position between two boulders with a clear view of the front gate.

John said, "From the sound of the machine gun fire earlier, it's evident you guys saw what happened."

JM answered. "Yeah. We saw. I wanted to shoot to kill, but Paul had given me clear instructions on when and how to use this thing. Did Paul make it?"

John looked at JM and the farmhand in turn and slowly answered, "No. He's dead."

The farmhand said, "I figured as much when I saw him drop. Man, he was such a great guy. I can't believe this has happened."

John looked to JM and said, "We've got work to do now. JM, Kent sent me to find you to ask you a question. The phone lines are dead, and the antenna for the shortwave radio has been disabled. We haven't been able to call out for help. We'd like to send someone up on the ridge with a cell phone to try to reach Sheriff Baylor or someone else for help and if that doesn't work to ride out on horseback for help. Kent wanted to know who you'd suggest we send."

"Normally, I'd go, but I think I'm gonna have to stay put here with this machine gun. We're the only ones who Paul trained on it. You know, Cal's down at the guard shack now. He's gone out on security with us. He could try to make the call. But if that doesn't work, then I'd suggest he go out on my mule, Rosebud. I assume this would be done shortly after it gets dark. Rosebud is the most surefooted animal we have and would get Cal where he needs to be. If Cal is willing, have him ease up here later. I'd like to talk with him before he heads out."

John agreed that Cal would be a good choice. "Okay. After I report back to Kent, one of us will talk to Cal about tonight. If he agrees, we'll have him come up to see you in a little bit. After losing his mother so recently, Kent may be reluctant to have his brother go on what could be a very dangerous mission."

"We'll be here," JM assured John.

"Yeah, we're not going anywhere," the farmhand replied.

Kent went over to the farmhouse and motioned for Sarah to follow him. He walked her over to a spot on the porch and asked her to sit in one of the rocking chairs.

Sarah asked, "What's going on? I know everyone's on alert, and we heard some gunfire in the distance. I'm sure I heard the sound of a machine gun too."

Kent hesitated and then said, "Sarah, I don't know how to tell you this except to come right out and say it."

"What? What's wrong? Is it Paul?" Sarah said with a look of dread on her face.

Kent looked directly into Sarah's eyes and said, "The people that pulled up had rifles and shot Paul in the back." Tears welled in Kent's eyes as he said, "Paul is dead." It was hard for Kent to watch as Sarah physically and emotionally collapsed in the chair where she sat.

Sarah wondered, *how could this happen after a career in the military working as a Special Forces noncommissioned officer and placing himself in harm's way on so many occasions? He was wounded a couple of times, earning him the Purple Heart. He then built a life farming a short commute from Fort Bragg, where he had spent much of his military career. Then he built a new life in Haven to live in safety, only to be shot down by some lowlife who knows nothing about duty, honor, and country.*

"I wanted to personally tell you, Sarah. I feel partly to blame." Kent then described what had happened, how they had both gone down to talk with the men who had driven up demanding that they all leave, how the property had been condemned. He told her how Paul had insisted that he, Kent, should go and get John for his legal opinion only as a ruse to get him to safety, how Paul apparently had decided to resolve things as best he could before John and he could return. "I'm one hundred percent convinced that Paul made a conscious decision to keep John and me from going back beyond the gate and in so doing sacrificed his life so that we could live. These are bad men we are dealing with. They have no scruples and won't think twice about killing all of us to get what they want."

"Let's just give it to them so that they'll go away," Sarah said through her tears.

"Sarah, I believe Paul would want us to protect ourselves. Otherwise, why would he have taken the action he did? Paul had courage."

Sarah agreed. "I know. He'd never back down from helping his friends and neighbors."

Kent knew that Paul was a man of strong character. "You're right."

"What are we going to do, Kent?" Sarah asked.

"We're going to hold on. We're going to do as Sheriff Baylor suggested if we can and not kill anyone, even though they deserve to be killed. The phone lines have apparently been cut and the radio antenna disabled. We suspect that the bad guys snuck onto the property and disabled the antenna shortly before they pulled up to the main gate. We're going to send someone up on the ridge to try to get service on a cell phone to call for help. Otherwise, someone will ride out of here and go for help."

"What do we do in the meantime?" Sarah was afraid not only for herself but for everyone in Haven.

Kent said, "You should go and rest. You need some time alone. I'll get someone else to watch dad."

Sarah quickly responded, "No. I think Paul would have me work now and mourn later. What can I do to help?"

Kent responded, "I think you should take some time."

Sarah was insistent. "Tell me what I should do."

Kent gave in. "Okay. Get dad. I want the both of you to get up to the lodge until this is over. I don't want him coming out and getting involved in this."

Sarah answered with a tone that meant business. "We'll get up there right away. You can count on me. Kent, I'm glad you're all right."

John approached the front gate, keeping his position directly behind the guard shack so that he would not be visible to the enemy across the way as he approached. John got Cal's attention.

"Cal, we can't make any calls out. The phone lines apparently have been cut. And as you already know, we can't call out on the shortwave because the antenna has been disabled. We need someone to ride up to the ridge line and attempt to call out on a cell phone, and if a call can't be made then to ride on into town for help. I asked JM who we should send; and he said he would normally go, but it turns out that he and one of the farmhands are manning the machine gun that was fired earlier. JM said they needed to stay on the gun but suggested that you are the best suited for the job due to your riding skills.

I know your brother won't really want you to go, but JM really thinks you're the best person for the task. Is that something you think you're up for?"

Cal nodded as he said, "Sure. I've ridden security a few times on patrol, and I'm more familiar with the property than anyone except maybe Kent."

John wanted to give Cal a moment to reconsider his decision. "Before you agree, I want you to know that there may be some bad guys up on the ridge. We think they were responsible for disabling the antenna that is up there. It may be dangerous, and you wouldn't be starting until after dark."

"I want to do it," Cal confidently replied.

John could see that Cal had no hesitation. "All right, we'll have someone down to relieve you from guard duty in a little bit. JM wants to talk with you before you leave. See those two boulders back up there?"

Cal looked up the mountain to where John was pointing. "Yes."

John explained. "JM and the farmhand are between those boulders. Once you've let the guards know you're going to be gone, ease your way over to them. Try not to draw any attention from the bad guys. We don't want them to know the location of the machine gun."

Cal understood the instructions. "All right, as soon as I'm relieved, I'll go up there."

John was afraid of what might happen when Cal reached the ridge line. John said, "Thanks, and good luck in case I don't see you later. My prayers will be with you."

"Thanks for that. I'll do my best," Cal assured John.

John hurried back to the lodge to meet Kent, who was waiting in his office.

"Beast, we'd better all get out of here," one of the thugs said. "We hadn't talked about killing anybody. I can't believe you killed him."

Beast had already considered that, but the deed was done. Beast was more concerned about the disrespect he had been shown. "Like I said, you saw how he walked away. He didn't stop when I told him to either. He had it coming."

"Well, now we're all in a lot of trouble. If we stay here, we're sure to get caught."

"No. You've got that backward," Beast said in an exceptionally harsh tone. "If we leave, we're sure to be caught. They've been taking pictures and have a zoom lens. They have our pictures. We can't leave that camera here."

"Well, I don't like it."

Beast abruptly turned and faced his fellow intruder as if he were going to hit him. "Leave if you have no stomach for it. Just don't come back to me with any of your problems to solve," Beast demanded.

"I didn't say anything about leaving," the thug sheepishly replied.

Beast relaxed slightly. "All right then. Shut up and wait. We'll make our move when it's good and dark." Beast paused for a moment and then said, "And did we get this road blocked?"

"It's blocked," the thug said.

Beast said calmly, "Okay. Sit tight." Beast was already starting to have some doubts about the information he had received from some guy named Alexander. The guy had said something about the IRS but Beast hadn't got it straight exactly what the guy was referring to. He only knew that he'd been given information about this place. He'd cut the phone lines. He knew about the antenna for a short wave radio they had. And he knew where the valuables were stored. Why this man would give him all of this information and not want a cut of the action didn't make sense. *What's in it for him?* Beast wondered.

"John, did everything go okay?" Kent asked.

"Yes. I found out where the machine gun fire came from. It turned out that Paul had brought a fifty-caliber machine gun and had it stored along with some ammunition at the defensive position overlooking the gate. He had trained JM to operate it along with one of the farmhands feeding the ammunition. Don't worry. Paul trained them well. JM showed a lot of control by not killing the man who shot Paul in the back earlier."

Kent was surprised. "I can't believe that Paul didn't tell us about the machine gun."

It made sense to John. "Think about it, Kent. What would our group have done if they'd known about the machine gun? We wouldn't even allow handguns when we set Haven up."

Kent thought for a moment and replied, "Yeah. You're right. I hope he had a permit for it."

John knew Paul well enough to know that he did things by the book. "I'm sure he did. He wouldn't have had it if it weren't legal. That's just how Paul was. Anyway, JM suggested your brother for the job of going up on the ridge tonight and attempt making a cell phone call. If that doesn't work, then he'll ride on into town for help. Cal's going to meet with JM for some instructions before heading out."

Kent asked, "Couldn't you all find anyone else?"

John knew this wasn't going to set well. "Kent, I knew you wouldn't be excited about Cal being the one to go, but think about it, he's a great rider and knows the area better than anybody else."

"All right, I agree that Cal's the best choice. I'm just not happy about it," Kent added.

"How'd it go with Sarah?" John had been thinking about how Sarah would hold up after learning of Paul's death.

Kent sighed and then said, "She was obviously shaken but insisted on continuing her work. She said that that's what Paul would have wanted."

"She's one tough woman," John said.

"She is. You know she went through a lot over the years while Paul was on active duty, especially during the many deployments that he went on. John, would you make the rounds and let everyone know what's happened, what the plan is, and that dinner will be brought to them where they're at?" Kent asked.

"Other than trying to call for help or going for help, what is the plan other than what Cal will be attempting?"

Kent had thought things through. The options seemed limited. He said, "We have to defend ourselves until help arrives. We need to keep all of the defensive areas manned continuously until then. That means that half of the residents will need to be on duty while the other half rest and sleep. The ones assigned to each position can arrange their own schedules as long as their position is manned. Also, emphasize that we still want to try to keep from killing anyone, despite what has happened."

John was concerned about how those on security duty would respond to anything out of the ordinary. John suggested, "That might be hard to enforce. Their blood's going to boil when they hear that they shot Paul in the back if they haven't heard already."

"Emphasize it," Kent said sternly. "You know that we want to do all that we can to stay on the right side of the law, even if we don't agree with everything our government does."

John knew that Kent was right. "I agree. Anything else you want to talk about before I go?" John asked.

"Be careful. After you've made the rounds and gotten something to eat, look me up so that we can compare notes on what's going on."

John replied, "All right. I'll see you later."

CHAPTER NINE

Mr. Rivera couldn't believe that he was sitting out behind some rocks and trees, sitting and waiting. Waiting for what? He didn't know. He had come to the defensive position that he had been assigned during the planning. He had heard a gunshot and then some machine gun fire a while ago and wondered what was going on. Other than that, it had been quiet and seemed like another drill, except that the alarm that sounded was not the alarm for a drill. This had been called as if it was the real thing. He heard a rustling in the leaves and looked around to see John quietly approaching. John put his index finger up to his lips, motioning for him to remain silent. He waited for John to reach his position.

John crouched down next to Mr. Rivera and spoke quietly. "I'm going from position to position to bring everyone up-to-date on what's going on. This is not a drill. There are a group of armed men outside the front gate. They told Kent and Paul that we were to leave our property, that the property had been condemned. Paul and Kent had gone out to talk with the men. Paul then sent Kent to get me. Shortly after Kent was out of sight, Paul was coming back to the gate and one of the men shot Paul in the back. Paul is dead. The phone line's been cut, and the antenna for the shortwave radio has been disabled. After dark Cal's going up on the ridge to try to make a cell phone call. If that doesn't work, he's going to ride into town for help."

"Paul is dead?" Mr. Rivera couldn't believe what he had heard.

Mr. Rivera had second thoughts about having cut the phone lines to Haven. *What was I thinking?* he wondered. Though he'd come here under false pretense, it really turned out to be a nice place. The people had all been wonderful to him and his family. But Agent Booker had a lot of power. Though Rivera didn't have much to lose, Agent Booker had made threats against his brother. He said he would ruin him. He said his brother would spend at least ten years in prison with what Booker had found auditing his brother's financial records. He had no idea that all this was going to happen. Paul murdered. *Am I an accessory to murder?* Mr. Rivera wondered. *If anyone finds out what I've done, I'll go to prison. What would happen to my family?*

John answered, "Yes. He was killed."

Mr. Rivera's mind was racing, thinking of what could be done. "Why don't we just leave like they asked? We could get help and come back later."

John wasn't surprised at Rivera's reply given his temperament. "Do you really think they would let us all leave here alive, knowing that we could get help and come back?"

"You're probably right," Mr. Rivera said reluctantly.

"You know I'm right. They wanted to get us all together

and then ambush us. Then they could come in here and take everything they want and leave as quickly as they came."

"I see what you mean. So what should I do?" Mr. Rivera asked.

John had looked around. It appeared that no one was with Rivera. "You're not manning this position alone, are you?"

"No. He's just gone up to the lodge to use the restroom," Mr. Rivera answered.

John then gave Mr. Rivera his instructions. "When he gets back, you two need to come up with a schedule. One of you has to be here awake, watching all the time. If you see any intruders, fire three warning shots. That will alert the others to send help your way. And don't shoot to kill unless you have no other choice."

"I don't want to shoot anybody." Mr. Rivera wasn't even sure he could shoot someone.

John asked, "Will you tell all of this to your team mate when he gets back? We want everybody to know what's going on."

"Yes, I'll tell him. It should be any minute now," Mr. Rivera replied.

"Okay. I'm going to keep making the rounds and updating the others." John then quietly backed away from Mr. Rivera's position and headed for the next.

Sally's assigned position during drills was to be with the children. When this alert had sounded, she was already with them and continued their normal activities. She was able to keep the children occupied so that they wouldn't worry about what might be going on.

Sarah had accompanied Pappy to the lodge as Kent had requested. Kent and Cal's dad had been doing fairly well considering the drastic loss he'd just experienced. He and Vera had been married over fifty years. Sarah didn't mind looking out for him. She felt like a kindred spirit having just lost her husband to the intruders. They mourned together and brought comfort to each other.

Sarah was glad that she and Pappy had moved up to the lodge. It would be safer than the house and Sarah realized she needed to be where she could be easily located in the event that anyone needed medical care. Suddenly becoming a widow didn't relieve her of her obligation to help the other members of the community. It was her Christian obligation. Pappy would rather be taking a more active role in defending the property but understood why Sarah looked after him the way she did.

After his replacement arrived Cal had informed the guards at the gate that he was needed elsewhere. Once relieved of guard duty, he and Kent went to meet with JM at his defensive position. They had to walk up toward the lodge and then back to the position to keep from being visible to the enemy. As they approached, it was obvious that JM and the farmhand were serious about their duty. Kent waited to speak until he and Cal were at the position. They spoke quietly so as to avoid being heard from below.

Kent looked at JM and said, "I can't believe that you are manning a machine gun here."

JM's expression did not change. "Paul kept that between us, thinking that if the other residents had known, they'd have wanted him to get rid of it. Now I think they'll have a different opinion."

Kent agreed. "I'm sure they will, but that made me out

to be a liar when I told the sheriff that he had seen all of the weapons that Haven has."

"No, it wasn't a lie," JM said. "You did show him all of the weapons Haven has. This machine gun wasn't the property of Haven. It was the personal property of Paul. It's legal, and he had a license for it. A copy's there in the ammo box."

Kent let it go and continued. "Anyway, Cal has agreed to ride up on your mule after dark to try making a cell phone call. If that's not successful, he's going to keep riding on into town for help."

"That's right. I'm ready to go," Cal said, affirming what Kent had stated.

Kent then said, "John said you had some instructions for Cal before he goes."

"That's right." JM looked at Cal. "You know what's happened. You saw it. I've heard that the radio antenna is out. I'm thinking that they've got one or more people up on the ridge. This may be dangerous. Are you sure you want to do this?"

Cal was determined. "Yes. I want to do this. It has to be done."

"You know the box just inside the tack room?" JM asked.

"Yes," Cal answered.

JM leaned over toward Cal and quietly said, "There's a compass in there with a luminescent dial. Take that. I'd also take a pack with bedding, some food, and some water. I'd travel unarmed. You'll need to wait until after dark to head out. I wouldn't go the way we normally go up. They'd be expecting that if they're up there. I'd use the trail over to the right of the mill."

"I know the one," Cal said.

JM continued his instructions. "Then you know its steeper, but where it comes out is pretty well concealed from above and below. From there, I'd follow the compass going due west. I'd ride for a couple of hours. That should put you far enough away that you won't be discovered. I'd bed down for the night wherever seems best and then, at first light, ride southwest. I've not ridden that route, but from the map, it looks passable. If the terrain is consistent with that around here, I would think you should make the main road by noon. I wouldn't ride in sight of the road. The bad guys could have someone driving up and down it, looking for you. I'd shadow the road from a distance. When you see the town, I'd tie Rosebud up somewhere and casually walk into town. Try calling Sheriff Baylor first. Also, I'd go to Preacher's house. Do you know where he lives?"

Cal shook his head and said, "No. You'd think as long as we've known each other I would, but I've never had an occasion to go over to his place. He's always come here."

"I don't remember the address, but it's near the center of town," JM Said. "In one of Preacher's sermons, he talked about what life was like where he lived."

"I've got the address in my office," Kent said. "Cal, I'll bring it down to you at the barn while you're getting ready."

"Anything else I need to know?" Cal asked.

"Yeah, be easy on Rosebud. She's surefooted, but she's no racehorse. It's sure and steady with her."

"I know. I know. I've been on her before," Cal assured JM.

JM smiled slightly and said, "That's why I suggested you."

"I'm glad you did," Cal said. "This sitting and waiting is hard. I'd rather be doing something."

"You have been doing something," Kent said. "I assure you. You've been helping keep our community safe."

"You know what I mean," Cal replied.

"Yes. I know," Kent said. "John's working his way from position to position, getting everyone up-to-date on what's happened. Each of you already know. The only other thing everyone's being told is not to shoot anyone if there's any possible way to avoid doing so."

JM quickly responded, "I'd sure like to shoot that sorry excuse for a man down there who killed Paul."

"We all would," Kent said, "but we've got to do the right thing, what God would have us do and what's best for our community. We don't want any of our residents to go to jail when this whole thing is over either."

JM replied, "I know. That's pretty much the instructions we received from Paul when he was training us on the weapon. Paul gave us very specific instructions not only on how to use the machine gun but when to. He also insisted that we not shoot to kill unless we have no other choice."

"Paul was right," Kent said. "Cal, you go ahead and get ready. I want to go down and give the guards some instructions. Then I'll go back to the lodge and get Preacher's address and meet you at the barn."

"Okay. I'll see you in a little bit." Kent and Cal left the position to go about their respective duties.

"Tad, gather the guys together. It'll be dark soon. We need to talk about our plan," Beast said in his domineering way.

Tad went to each vehicle, telling everybody to come up and talk about what they were going to do. It only took a few minutes to get everyone together.

"Beast, we're ready," Tad said anxiously. Tad wouldn't have come, except that Pat was his brother and had shamed him into coming. Pat never liked his name and had taken to calling himself Beast since he started running with a bad group before dropping out of high school. He'd been caught robbing a convenience store and had done some hard time in prison. Since Beast was paroled, he'd been up to no good. Tad had never been able to stand up to his brother. Tad knew that he had made a bad choice in coming. There was no way he was going to get out of this; it was too late for that now.

Beast said in a commanding voice, "Okay. Here's what we're going to do. When it's dark, we'll start taking out these stumps. When they're all up, we'll get in the vehicles, turn around, and drive out like we're leaving. Then we'll turn around and come back. The first four trucks will get going real fast and drive right through the front gate. The others will stay on this side, and we'll have the people at the gate trapped. Once we're beyond the gate, we'll stop, get out, and kill the guards. Then we'll find that camera they were using and destroy it."

"How about the machine gun? They're sure to fire on us as we drive through," one of the other men said.

Beast answered, "They won't be able to see well enough after it gets dark to do much. Once we take out the guards, it should be pretty easy to sweep up the rest of the compound. Then we can go through everything and take what we can carry out of here."

Another man asked, "Don't you think they've found a way to call for help by now?"

"No. I coordinated through the guy that gave me the information on this place to have the phone line cut. I tried the number and got a message saying the line is out of service. That's not a problem. Also, our two guys up on the ridge took out the antenna for their shortwave radio, and there's no cell phone service in this valley. The boys are up on the ridge now to make sure that no one gets up there to try to get cell phone reception to make a call." Beast had had enough of the questions from his men and said with a look that made it clear that he wouldn't tolerate any backtalk, "Any other questions? Everybody, make sure your guns are loaded, and get ready. It won't be long now. You'll hear me start up my vehicle when it's time. Then we'll make our move."

Most of Beast's men were callous just like he was. They had little value for life and no appreciation for property rights. It was as if they had no understanding of the difference between right and wrong.

"Brother, I hope you know what you're getting yourself into," Kent said.

"You know this is the right thing to do," Cal replied.

"I wish I had your riding skills and could do this instead of you, Cal."

"Hey, little brother, you know I'm the one for this job. Now let's stop all of this talkin'. I need to get on the trail. See you when I get back." Cal reached out to shake his brother's hand.

Kent reached out his right hand and then reached around his brother with his left hand, pulling him close. "I love you, Cal. Godspeed."

"I love you too, man. See you soon."

With Preacher's address in hand, Cal started toward the mill right as it was getting dark. He didn't want to make the ascent until it was completely dark. The moon was out, but gave little light, as it was only about a third illuminated. Just as he decided to start up, he could feel his heart pounding in his chest and his neck muscles tense up. He was confident of his ability to ride up to the top of the ridge and on into town. What caused his stress was that he would be doing so in the dark with the possibility of armed men intent on stopping him at the top or anywhere along the way for that matter. Even so, he was committed to doing this. Paul had already given his life for them, and they were still at risk. He would let Rosebud set the pace up the mountain as long as she kept moving. He gave her the signal to start by applying light pressure, pulling his calves lightly against her sides. She started forward. When they arrived at the spot where it became steep, Cal stopped Rosebud and got off. He thought it would be best for Rosebud if he led her up on foot rather than force her to walk up the steepest part with the burden of carrying him. Rosebud could handle his weight. However, Cal felt safer walking, at least until they got to where it wasn't so steep.

It took nearly an hour to make it to the top. He took it slow and easy, stopping to listen every few minutes. Cal wouldn't have been able to do this when he first arrived in Haven. Before coming here, about the most physical activity he had was changing the toner cartridge in the copier in the office of his feed store. Since moving to Haven to help take care of his parents, Cal had been a jack-of-all-trades. Jean had helped him with the paper work. He'd supervised the ranch hands, and he'd spent time as a guard. None of these activities had been overly physical. But he had also spent a lot of time working with Paul, JM, and the others in the garden, mending fences, moving feed, digging post holes, chopping wood, and all of the other physical activities associated with farm work. He seemed a natural when it came to riding, though there were days when he would go to bed sore at first. He'd ridden a little when he was younger, but that had been a long time ago. At the top, Cal unsuccessfully tried the cell phone. He wasn't surprised that there was no service.

He remounted Rosebud and continued his journey. He would frequently check his compass as they moved quietly through the dark woods. He would take a few steps, stop, check the compass, and then look and listen for any sign of trouble. He'd repeat that process over and over until they were well away from the ridge line. When he heard movement, he'd sit tight and wait awhile. Off to his right, he heard a twig snap. His eyes had had plenty of time to adjust to the low light level. He sat on Rosebud there about twenty minutes until he saw what appeared to be a deer in the distance, slowly moving along the edge of the wood line. Cal relaxed slightly and resumed the slow forward progress.

According to the instructions JM had given him, Cal should be stopping for the night. However, Cal felt that he had been moving so slowly that he certainly hadn't covered the distance that JM had in mind, so he pressed on another hour, moving in the same manner. Cal had gotten sleepy a while back but seemed to have gotten a second wind. He was now fully alert again. Despite JM's instructions, Cal knew that time was of the essence, that the whole community was in jeopardy, and that he had an instrumental part to play in getting the help that was so desperately needed. He decided to forgo the stop for the rest of the night if he could and pressed on. He stopped and checked the compass again and reset the dial to southwest. That would take him out to the main road. There was a stream where he stopped, so he and Rosebud took a drink. After a short break, they moved on.

The guards had been hearing something going on out front, maybe digging. They had shined a spotlight out there briefly from time to time to try to see what was happening. Unfortunately, the first vehicle was parked in such a way as to completely obscure the view. They had left the light off most of the time so that they wouldn't present a target should the enemy decide to take pot shots at them. Later, they heard one of the vehicle's engines start up, followed by the others. The guards were prepared to blow the portion of the road that had remained after the ditch had been dug if the vehicle pulled forward toward it. They'd been instructed to blow the remaining portion of the road before a vehicle reached it so that no one would be hurt. One of the guards had his finger on the detonator, waiting to see what would happen.

Much to their surprise, the vehicles seemed to be turning around. They finally did turn around and then drove away. They all felt a great sense of relief until one of them turned the spotlight on and looked down the road. Their relief turned into apprehension when they saw that the barricades had been removed. Then they heard the sound of vehicles approaching and it sounded like they were coming fast. As soon as the lead truck was seen coming out of the bend in the road heading for the gate, the detonator was pushed, and the only entryway for vehicles in and out of Haven was gone in an instant.

Beast saw the road going up in front of him. Part of the blast sent debris into the windshield. He slammed on the brakes, trying to stop before reaching the blast area. The momentum of the vehicle kept the vehicle moving forward until the front wheels dropped into the depression the blast had made. After the front of the truck hit the far side of the ditch with a thud, the rear end of the truck lifted up and then dropped back down. Beast's body was flung headfirst through the windshield, leaving his lifeless body laying half in and half out of the truck. His brother had had the sense to wear his seatbelt. Even so, he hit his head on the windshield, dazing him momentarily; but he quickly got out of the vehicle and hurried back to the other trucks that had escaped colliding with theirs.

The others got out of their vehicles and came over to Tad. The one that went by the name Bone Crusher asked, "Where's Beast?" Tad liked to think of himself as being next in command after his brother, but he knew that Bone Crusher would take over. It wasn't an accident he was called Bone Crusher.

"He's in the truck. He's dead," Tad answered.

Bone Crusher was visibly upset. "They're going to pay for this," he said as he hit the fist of one hand into the palm of the other. "Here's what we're gonna do. We're gonna drive the trucks back beyond the bend out of site. Then half of us are going to walk into the ditch way over on one side and then come around back to where the guards are. They won't be expecting us there. The others will be out on this side, using the trees as cover, some on one side of the road and some on the other. Then we'll open fire and put an end to them. Tad, I'll take my boys to the other side. You can spread the others out here. When you hear us open fire, you all join in. Got it?"

Several of the men echoed, "Got it."

"Okay. Let's go," Bone Crusher ordered.

JM and the farmhand had intently watched everything that had gone on below. Despite JM's strong desire to open fire, he maintained control and held back. He felt an obligation to following the instructions that Paul had given him concerning when to fire and the importance of keeping his position concealed. They would sit tight and wait. This was not over yet.

The guards were surprised to hear the vehicles start up and turn around again. They drove out of sight. Then everything seemed normal, except for the truck sitting in the ditch where the road had been. They shined a light out toward the front. It was unsettling for them to see a lifeless body hanging out of the windshield. One of them called on the field phone. This time there was an answer. They reported all that had happened in the last few minutes to Kent and told him that one of the intruder's had been killed when his truck slid into the newly formed ditch. Kent was disappointed to hear about that but warned the guards to stay alert. They were all certain that they hadn't seen the last of the bad guys. Kent asked John's wife to position herself at the gate with the guards. He asked her to let some of the dogs out to monitor security along the ditch. Without the dogs, it would be relatively easy to bypass the gate on foot and catch the guards by surprise.

Cal's head began nodding from lack of sleep. His eyelids suddenly felt heavy. If Cal was reading Rosebud right, she was getting a little sleepy too. Cal didn't want to stop, so he decided a change of pace might help. He dismounted and walked for a while. Maybe the physical exertion would wake him back up and give Rosebud some needed rest. Rosebud hadn't been ridden this far as long as Cal had known her.

As Cal's blood began moving, his senses returned. He checked the compass. He was still moving in the right direction. It shouldn't be long until he came to the main road and be able to follow it into town. Though the moon wasn't full, the stars were in all their glory. It would be easy to get distracted admiring God's creation if the mission that Cal was on wasn't so vital. Up ahead, Cal could see a glow on the horizon. He knew that he couldn't be seeing the last light of the setting sun. That had long ago dipped below the horizon. It had to be the glow from the lights in town. Even with the lights in view, it was impossible to determine how far remained until help could be summoned.

Somewhere in the distance, Cal could hear the familiar whoosh of a passing vehicle, *but how far?* Cal wondered. Cal knew that sound was a funny thing. Where he had lived before, he normally couldn't hear the expressway off in the distance. There were times that it sounded annoyingly close. There were other times that he could hear voices that seemed nearby. However, he knew they could only be coming from his neighbors far across the fields. It made him think of the time he was sightseeing in a large church where you could stand in one spot and a friend in a spot at the far side of the church. You would whisper and your friend could distinctly hear what you had said. Cal knew that he was heading in the right direction but was uncertain how far was left to travel.

Make town by daylight. That was what Cal was trying to do. He continued to try the cell phone, but still there was no reception. He felt more relaxed now. He was fully awake again, and Rosebud seemed to be her old self. So Cal decided to mount up again and ride for a ways. Suddenly, he could hear the sound of another creek. As he approached it, he saw its shadowy form beneath the pines and decided against crossing it unless he had to. He decided to follow its course. With the lay of the land being what it was, he was certain that it would intersect the main road and that crossing it without the benefit of a bridge wouldn't be necessary. He and Rosebud plodded on.

Deep down Tad was glad that Bone Crusher had taken charge, even though he despised him. Tad didn't have the stomach for what now needed to be done. If it hadn't been for his brother, they wouldn't be in this mess. If he had only taken his brother's ridicule and stayed home, he wouldn't be facing the very real possibility of being a guest at the state's penal institution, his brother's recent home away from home.

After taking time to have a couple of drinks, Bone Crusher had mustered the courage to lead some of the men across the ditch that he had instructed the men about earlier. It was time. He pointed to some of them seated nearby. "Okay. You four guys follow me. The rest of you, wait until you hear us open fire. Then spread out and come over and attack the guards with us. After we've taken them out, we'll search for the camera. Let's move."

The four men looked back and forth at each other and then

at Bone Crusher. His eyes were fixed on them. They knew that if they didn't promptly comply, they would have to deal with him. They'd rather deal with the guards at the gate, so they grabbed their guns and stood up. At that point, they moved in unison toward the north slope of the hill at the far end of the ditch. They moved as quietly as they could.

"Now. Let's cross now," Bone Crusher ordered.

As soon as they had eased their way into the ditch, they heard movement on the far side. They stood frozen in place, listening.

After a couple of minutes, Bone Crusher whispered, "It was nothing. Let's get going."

Bone Crusher placed his free hand on the top of the ditch. With his other hand firmly grasping his pistol, he placed it beside the other. He then started to pull himself up when he heard movement again and then a dog bark. It wasn't the sound of a dog off in the distance. This dog was barking close, like it was on the scent of a fresh meal. Then there was the sound of at least two or more dogs barking.

The men with Bone Crusher stopped as suddenly as he did; however, after taking a quick glance at each other, they turned around, quickly mounting the ledge they had just descended. Feeling a bit safer there, they stopped, waiting for Bone Crusher to join them and give them further instructions.

After Bone Crusher realized that he was alone in the ditch, and not being any too fond of dogs, he too retreated to his former position atop the bank of the ditch. He didn't comment on the men's hasty retreat. He stood dumbfounded, thinking of what to do next. He knew that the dogs would have the advantage in the dark. Otherwise, he and his men could easily take them out. He motioned for the men to follow him back to their starting position. The others had heard the dogs as well. They all had an eerie feeling listening to the sound of dogs barking so close on a dark night. It was what they would have imagined as more fitting for a nightmare than real life.

Bone Crusher didn't let their fears linger for long; he shouted out orders that they would shift positions to attack from the other side if they weren't met by the dogs. After repeating the same procedures as before, they were met with the same result: vicious sounding dogs barking just up ahead.

After retreating again to the starting point, Bone Crusher instructed the men that they would now have to wait for first light so they could take out the dogs before crossing the ditch. This meant that they would again be faced with coming under machine gun fire in the light of day. That prospect didn't settle well with the men. Bone Crusher hadn't heard anything from up on the ridge and presumed that all was going well there. Now there was nothing to do but wait for morning.

Since the residents of Haven had to continue in their protective posture, the children weren't able to go to their families at the end of the day like they had always done before. Sally had told the children that she had gotten special permission for them to have a lock-in. Some of the children weren't familiar with what a lock-in was. When she explained the term, they were thrilled. It was like a slumber party. Sally had been thinking out activities throughout the day in preparation should the trouble not be resolved by then. They were going to be given parts and put on a play based on a Bible story that they selected. If available, Pappy and Sarah had volunteered to be their audience. Later, they would all have popcorn and watch a movie. Sally's plan was to keep the kids busy until they were exhausted and fell asleep on their own.

Frankly, Sally needed to keep her mind occupied too. She loved Sarah and she felt terrible that Sarah was going to have to go on without Paul. It wasn't fair. She wondered if this was going to shake Sarah's faith. It certainly would hers. She knew that her faith wasn't as strong as her sister Barb's. Oh, she believed but just wasn't certain that God took an active role in her life. She thought that maybe he was more of a judgmental observer than an active participant. She had talked about this with her and was trying to understand spiritual things the way she did. Hopefully, in time, she would.

The kids enjoyed putting on the play for their audience. They certainly weren't ready to take it on the road, but the spirit was there and they had a great time. Sally didn't know what Pappy and Sarah had really thought of it, but they were a fine audience and gave the children a standing ovation at the end. They even stayed and enjoyed watching the movie with them.

The children had long since fallen asleep. Sally, Pappy and Sarah kept each other company, dozing off sometimes and sitting quietly at others. They had only briefly talked about Paul. The subject was too painful for them to deal with for any length of time.

The guards, John's wife, JM, and the farmhand were all fretfully waiting on what would come next. They'd take turns catching what sleep they could. Across the ditch, those opposing them were spending their time in the same manner. They weren't concerned with what would come from across the ditch. Rather, they were concerned on what might come off the main road toward them. They had the road blocked, but that didn't guarantee they wouldn't have company. They too seized what sleep their nervous minds would allow them, waiting on Bone Crusher to give the next orders at first light.

Some of the men would have preferred to slip off in the

dark and try to pretend that none of this had ever happened, but after considering their options, they decided to stay. They were convinced that if they weren't caught by the law, Bone Crusher would track them down and finish them off. There would be no jury trial and no lawyers working to help them with Bone Crusher. Falling into the hands of law enforcement would be preferable to those of Bone Crusher. They waited in silence.

It wouldn't be long until daybreak. Cal was right. The stream did intersect the main road. He rode across the bridge and then back off the road. He then began following it toward town. The radiant light from town was growing. Cal had followed JM's instructions and stayed off the road after crossing the creek, though this made for slower going. He would be stopping soon and tying Rosebud up in a secure spot. He tried the cell phone one last time. He opened the cover. His hopes swelled after hearing the sound indicating service was available. He dialed Sheriff Baylor's number. He lost the signal. He tried again and then tried 911 before closing the cell phone and putting it away. As he approached the outskirts of town, he looked for a good spot to leave Rosebud. He wanted to make sure that she would be all right until he could come back for her. After giving the matter a lot of thought as he looked for a place, he decided against following that portion of JM's instructions. He knew how much Rosebud meant to JM and didn't want to take a chance on someone hurting, killing, or stealing JM's beloved mule.

Cal decided that rather than walking to Preacher's house, he would find the first house he could that looked like they would be up and willing to let him try placing a phone call. He hoped the phone lines were working in town. When Cal reached the outskirts, he bypassed the main road, where he would have been easily seen. He opted to enter on a side road, a road that became a dirt trail after passing the last house. He dismounted and led Rosebud as they passed several houses. Cal saw lights on in one and could hear someone talking through the open window. He tied Rosebud's reigns around a fence post and walked up to the porch. He stood for a moment listening and then climbed the steps, knocked on the front door, and took a couple of steps back so that he wouldn't look intimidating when someone answered.

Cal could see that someone had pulled the curtains back slightly to peek out. He knocked again and waited. After about a minute, Cal heard what sounded like an elderly man holler out from behind the unopened door, "What do you want? I've got a gun, and I'm not afraid to use it." He then heard the distinctive sound of a pump shotgun having a shell placed in the chamber.

"I need help. I need to place a phone call. It's an emergency."

"I'm not going to let you in no matter what you say. You be on your way now, you hear?" the old man said, the sound of fear in his voice.

"I don't mean to be a bother, but people's lives are at stake." Cal didn't want to mention that he was from Haven on the off chance that he might be giving himself away to someone that was in league with the bad guys, but he felt that there was no way that this man was a part of that so he did. "My name is Cal Davidson. I've come from Haven. Our phone lines have been cut, and some bad men have killed one of the members of our community. The bad men were still there when I left last night to get help. See, the mule I rode out on is tied up down by the road. Please," Cal pleaded with the man. "I've got to call for help."

"My wife and I don't let people in during the middle of the night. I can't help you," the man said sternly.

"How about you make the call for me? I can give you

the number, and you can call and tell them Cal Davidson's outside."

"I guess there's no harm in that. Who do you want me to call?" the man asked.

"Call Sheriff Baylor." Cal then gave him the number.

"Okay, I'll call. Sit in the rocking chair, and don't try anything. I'll have an eye on you while I try the number."

"I'll be right here. I'm sorry to bother you so early in the morning. I appreciate your help." As Cal sat down in the rocking chair, he silently prayed to God that the man would be able to reach Sheriff Baylor.

Sheriff Baylor had gone out to dinner with his wife the night before and had been looking forward to sleeping in. He hadn't had a day off in a while and was anxious to catch up on some much-needed rest. About an hour before sunrise, the phone rang. Sheriff Baylor thought about letting it go to voice mail but knew that he couldn't. A call coming at this time of day would undoubtedly be some kind of emergency. Despite the phone ringing, Sheriff Baylor's wife didn't move. Over the years, she had become accustomed to the phone ringing at all times of the day or night.

He answered, "Hello. This is Sheriff Baylor."

"Sheriff, I have a man on my porch that says he's got an emergency."

"Let me talk with him," Sheriff Baylor responded.

"I don't want to let him in my house. My wife and I are old, and we don't let people in after dark, no matter what," the man said.

"Well, who is it, and what's the emergency?" Sheriff Baylor asked.

"The man says his name is Cal Davidson, and he's from

the place up in the mountains called Haven. He said a man's been murdered, and there are bad people still there."

"I know Cal. Please let me talk to him," Sheriff Baylor asked.

"Hold on," the man replied. "The man walked to the door and hollered out, "I'm going to unlock the door. I'm going to stand back with my gun on you. Come in if you want and talk to the sheriff. Then, when you're done, go back out and close the door behind you."

"Thank you." Cal got up and walked to the door and waited for a moment so the man wouldn't be startled. Cal didn't want to get shot after all this. After he was certain that the man would be ready, he gently opened the door and slowly walked in. He saw the phone lying off the hook on a table by a chair. He walked over and picked up the receiver. "Sheriff Baylor, this is Cal Davidson from Haven. Paul's been murdered."

"Hold on a minute." Sheriff Baylor got up out of bed and walked to the living room. He turned the light on, sat down, and picked up the phone there. "Paul's been murdered you say?"

"Yes. Murdered by some men who pulled up to the front gate. They said our property was condemned and ordered us to leave. After they had finished talking to Paul and he was walking back to the gate, they shot him in the back. I left after dark on JM's mule and rode into town. They apparently cut the phone lines and disabled our shortwave radio antenna, and of course, our cell phone didn't work. Even when I got up on the ridge and all the way into town I couldn't get service. They need help. As far as I know, the bad guys are still there, holding our community hostage."

"I'll call for back up and get over there right away," Sheriff Baylor assured Cal.

"Sheriff, I wouldn't go in alone. There may be up to twenty or so of the bad guys."

"Thanks for the heads up. I'll call headquarters and explain what's going on. We'll coordinate our arrival and come in force as quick as we can make it happen. Where will you be?"

"Now that I'm in town and have reached you, I plan on going to Preacher's house. I'll be there." Cal then gave him Preacher's address and phone number in case Sheriff Baylor needed it later.

"I'm sorry to hear about Paul. Don't worry. We'll get help there soon." Sheriff Baylor immediately called headquarters and started planning for what would follow.

CHAPTER TEN

As the guards' anxiety continued to grow, the faintest of light could be seen developing in the eastern sky. They had been thankful for John's wife and her dogs, but as dawn approached, they became more and more uneasy contemplating what might happen next. Something had to happen. This couldn't go on forever. They joined in prayer together. They prayed that God would protect their community, keep Cal safe, and bring help. Thoughts drifted to Cal and his going for help. *Did he make it out? Has he been killed too?* All of these thoughts swirled around their collective minds. It had become a lonely and frightening outpost at what seemed to be the end of the world. *Would we have been better off had we not come to Haven? No one forced us to come.*

JM had been dozing while the farmhand remained on watch. Having gone through so much in his life, JM was better able to deal with the prospect of getting some rest despite the uncertainty of what the future held, let alone the next few minutes. The farmhand, on the other hand, was wide-eyed in fearful anticipation. He felt the rush of adrenaline like he felt when he'd gone deer hunting in the past with his father. However, this was mixed with an equal dose of fear, uncertain of what would soon take place. He knew it was time for JM to take watch while he rested, *but what's the point?* he wondered. There would be no rest for him now. He decided to let JM slumber a while longer. JM had proved his mettle through this ordeal. If it wasn't for his appearance, you would never know that he was getting on in years. He had to admit, he admired JM for his determination to see this thing through and do his part. As far as he was concerned, JM was doing more than his part.

Back at the lodge, everything was quiet. The children, worn out and tired from their late night activities, had fallen asleep long ago. Pappy was sprawled out on a couch and was resting comfortably. Sarah had leaned back in an overstuffed chair next to a coffee table where she was sleeping lightly. She felt restless being sequestered away from where the trouble was brewing. She decided to go over to Kent's office and trying calling for help again, though she knew what the results would be before she picked up the receiver. She had to do something. She picked up the receiver. Nothing happened. Sarah restlessly paced the office, feeling a sense of helplessness. She knew she was where she needed to be; but to her, it didn't seem like she was making a contribution toward the problem at hand. She prayed that no one would be hurt or worse. She prayed that her medical skills wouldn't be needed. She knelt by the desk and prayed for what seemed like a miracle.

Two of the thugs were still up on the ridgeline waiting for something to happen. They were a father and son team up to no good. They had jumped at the chance to be a part of this. They had taken turns watching below. They had taken care of the antenna easily enough. They were pretty sure that no one had bypassed them. They were wondering why things were taking so long. Junior thought for certain that they would be in control shortly after dark at the latest. *What is happening?* he wondered. Junior was grown and had had a few scrapes with the law, nothing serious though. Usually he was picked up as any easy scapegoat for whatever had happened, at least that's the way it was if you listened to him.

With Junior was his father who had had the same experience as a young man. With age, he had become more cunning in making his choices. Take tonight for example. He wasn't down below where he could get caught if something went wrong but where he could sweep down to share in the plunder when the time came. Off in the distance, he could make out what looked like a snake of red and blue lights winding its way far off coming in their direction. He gave his boy a nudge.

Junior sat up and exclaimed, "What, Dad?"

His dad pointed toward the light show that had developed in the distance. It wasn't long until they could hear the unmistakable faint sound of sirens.

"I think it's time we hightail it out of here," his father said.

"I'm with you, Dad. Let's go."

They got up, packed their gear, and made a hasty retreat the way they had come through the national forest. They both wanted to be long gone when the fireworks lit up down below.

Those on both sides of the gate didn't have the vantage point that the two up on the ridge had. Those on the ridge had seen the lights coming—trouble to the men on the outside of the gate and rescue for those inside. The way the sound traveled during the wee hours of the morning, those manning the road block were the first down below to hear the sirens. After thinking more about their situation, they weren't as afraid of Bone Crusher as they originally thought. Maybe he would be captured or killed and they wouldn't have to worry about him. Knowing that Beast was dead gave them courage to go against the instructions Bone Crusher had given them. They hopped in their vehicles and sped away, leaving the road open and cutting the number of men standing with Bone Crusher against those in Haven. Due to the terrain, the sound of the fleeing vehicles couldn't be heard by Bone Crusher and the men with him. They had the false sense of security thinking that the other guys had their back.

Bone Crusher was giving the last-minute instructions, preparing for the assault that would be made at first light. His instructions were that they would split up into two groups, half crossing the ditch on opposite sides of the road near where the ditch met the rise in the hill. Once they entered the ditch, they would hold up and listen for the dogs. Bone Crusher made sure that each group had a sawed-off shotgun to use when they were confronted by the dogs again. The group led by Tad would enter the ditch, first attempting to divert attention of both the guards and the men on the machine gun. Bone Crusher's group would enter on the side of the road that lay below where they thought the machine gun fire had come from. Their initial objective was to take out the machine gun. After that, they would double back toward the gate and join Tad's group in attacking the guards. Then they would search for the camera. Finally, they would kill the rest of the community and take everything that they had originally come for. Bone Crusher was confident that all would go well once they got past the machine gun.

Cal was relieved that he had been able to reach Sheriff Baylor so soon. By taking the initiative to alter the original plan, Cal had accelerated the notification process by several hours. He felt rather foolish leading Rosebud down city streets as he headed toward Preacher's house. However, he was so tired it really didn't matter. He was nearly there. *Two more blocks to go. One more. There it was.* Cal tied Rosebud's reigns to a low-hanging limb, walked up the front steps, and lightly tapped on the door. As he had done previously, he then stepped back so that he could be easily seen should the Preacher or his wife look out to see who was calling so early in the morning.

This time, the door swung open, and Preacher said, "Good morning, Cal. Kind of early to be making a house call, don't you think? Come on in, sit down, and tell my why you're here."

Cal entered Preacher's living room. He had never been to Preacher's home before. It was simply furnished but had a comfortable feel to it. It was simple but tastefully decorated. Cal apologized for the early hour of his calling and then proceeded to tell Preacher about what had taken place since yesterday. Preacher was obviously saddened when he heard that Paul had been killed. However, he was glad to know that Sheriff Baylor had been contacted and was on the way with help. Preacher told Cal that he'd like to lead them in prayer for the residents at Haven, to pray that God would protect them. Cal readily agreed. After the prayer was complete, Preacher suggested that they try to contact the sheriff, which Cal was anxious to do. After calling his office, they were patched directly to Sheriff Baylor's car. Sheriff Baylor told them they were just arriving at the turnoff to Haven from the main road. He'd have to hang up and talk to them later. There was work to be done now.

Once the phone call was complete, Cal and Preacher heard the unmistakable sound of a mule. "Oh, Preacher, while we wait, I think I should give Rosebud a drink and some feed. We brought some feed with us, but I'd appreciate it if I could get a bucket of water for her. We've both had a hard night."

"After we get her settled, I think it would be best if you make yourself comfortable in our guest bedroom, first door on the left as you go down the hall. The bathroom's the next door on the left. I hope you don't take offense, but you might want to take a shower too."

"No offense taken," Cal replied. "It'll be hard to sleep waiting to hear what's happening in Haven, but it's going to be hard to stay awake too. I'll take you up on your offer. After I feed and water Rosebud, I'll take a shower and then lay in bed for a while."

The sound of emergency vehicles could now be heard echoing between the hills and carrying on up to the lodge. Everyone in Haven who was awake felt the hope rise in them that help was on the way. As time passed, their hopes were confirmed as they could see the lights reflecting through the valley from the police and other emergency vehicles approaching the entryway to Haven. Sheriff Baylor was in the lead vehicle as they came to an abrupt stop behind those of Bone Crusher and his bunch. Due to the geography of the valley, Bone Crusher hadn't been able to hear the approaching convoy until they had turned off the main road, trapping him and the others between those approaching from the main road in one direction and the guards, dogs, and machine gun in the other.

Sheriff Baylor was livid at the thought of these hoodlums shooting Paul in the back. His adrenaline was pumping as he turned off the main road and drove toward the gate. When he pulled up and saw the vehicles stopped on the road in front, he thought about what might have been going on for most of the last twenty-four hours. The younger men on the force had a high sense of anticipation. They had only received a little information on what was going on but enough to know it was something big. Most had not seen real action before and were still imagining the heroic scenes they had seen in the movies or stories they had heard from their seniors. They were disappointed when they saw some of the criminals approaching them unarmed with their hands in the air. They relieved their frustrations to some extent through their rough handling of them. One or two prisoners were placed in the back of each patrol car.

Some of Bone Crusher's younger men broke ranks at a jog away from the road and scampered up the hillside, hoping to hike out to safety before they were discovered. Others recognized the hopelessness of the situation and resigned themselves to being arrested. They threw their guns down, held their hands up, and walked slowly and deliberately back to where they had started by their vehicles. Before they could reach their vehicles, they were approached by what they pictured as storm troopers. They were roughly treated as they were bodily turned around and pushed flat on their stomachs on the ground. Their hands were then pulled behind their backs as they were frisked and then unceremoniously handcuffed.

Bone Crusher and Tad knew they had nothing to lose so they took off. Tad headed down the length of the ditch and started climbing up the mountain. They would both be prominently pictured in the photos taken by the guard. Tad knew that he would be charged for murder no differently than if he had personally pulled the trigger. Tad thought back on his brother with hatred. If he'd have only stood up to him, he wouldn't be in this position. He might have been beaten and bruised by him, but that wouldn't be anything compared to the treatment that he would be receiving in prison. From what his brother had told him, prison was tough. If it was tough for his brother, he knew it would be tougher for him. Tad was much smaller than his brother and didn't have the intimidating presence his brother had. After dwelling on these matters for a moment, he followed the others that were trying to make their escape on foot.

In didn't take long for Bone Crusher to realize that he was alone, it had become each man alone to fend for himself. Those stinking cowards wouldn't stand up and fight. There was nothing else to do. He couldn't accomplish anything alone, so he headed away from the standoff, seeking a way to quietly sneak out. He followed in the direction that Tad had taken. With the incriminating photos the guard had, he would have to keep on going and never look back.

As Cal fell asleep, Preacher had gone into his study and dropped to his knees. He started praying fervently for his congregation, for his friends in Haven. He remained in that posture, praying, beseeching the Lord to keep them and those who had come to rescue them safe.

Sheriff Baylor crossed the ditch, walked over to the guard shack, and learned that several of the people that had come to attack Haven had run up into the mountains, trying to escape on foot. John's wife approached Sheriff Baylor and suggested that the dogs could be used to start tracking them down, especially if they started right away. He tried to dissuade her. He knew that it would be dangerous. Those men would be armed and not afraid to use their weapons. She was insistent, suggesting that each guard take a dog and that the sheriff's men accompany them. After considering the proposal, he decided it would be a good idea to at least know in what direction the human refuse were taking. By knowing that, he could send patrol cars out to intercept them as they reached the road. That would put the bad guys in a box, hopefully motivating them to give up without a fight. He agreed and said they'd be set up in five minutes to start the search.

When Sheriff Baylor arrived back at his vehicle, he called out and requested that helicopters be deployed to his location if any were available. He learned that a news helicopter was already en route, having heard some information on the police channel that piqued their interest. Sheriff Baylor's call was relayed to the pilot. He requested that the pilot begin a search for the fleeing criminals by flying out in a circular pattern until people were viewed below and then call in to report their position. He also instructed them to stay at a high altitude so as to avoid being shot at.

John's wife quickly arrived with two guards and the cook in the company of four dogs, providing four teams to begin the search. The two guards had never gone off duty, knowing that they were desperately needed where they were. They had been joined by the cook who was the least experienced dog handler, but John's wife had given him some quick instructions that she was sure would get him through. She had paired him up with Ivy, a strong Belgium Malinois, because she was a natural and could nearly do the job without the help of a human handler. The guards had Goldie and Speckles, who were both well-trained and ready for the job. She would take Buster, the most timid of the four, but the best tracker of the bunch.

"Sheriff, we're ready," she said as the dogs and handlers were each matched up with the patrolmen.

"Just a minute and I'll have the men ready to go with you. They each have two-way radios that should work well unless you get down in some hollow, so get up on high ground and try contacting us again if you have problems reaching me. I'll be coordinating the information you give me to men that I'll have prepositioned to intercept the criminals that are fleeing. They'll be fanned out around this valley on the roads that the criminals are most likely to come out on. Do you have any idea how many we're looking for?"

One of the guards answered, "We saw about twenty people at first, but they sent some away, and others have already turned themselves in. I think maybe a dozen or so are left."

Sheriff Baylor gave the instructions. "Now, I don't want you to get too far ahead. This may very well be dangerous. You'll each have three patrolmen with you. When I got the call, I contacted the state highway patrol and asked for additional assistance. We've jointly come to help resolve this matter." Sheriff Baylor matched each of the dog handler's up with the patrolmen that would accompany them as they moved out. If the numbers were right, it would be four teams searching for about a dozen people. Those weren't good odds, but the eyes in the sky would help even the odds along with the police officers scattered along the roads waiting on instructions on where to intercept the criminals.

Each of the dog handlers gave the dogs the signal to start when they reached the base of the hills at the far ends of the ditch. Each of the dogs picked up a scent and got to work right away, eagerly pulling their handlers along behind them. Each team was headed in different directions as they started up. The dogs were all barking as they had when they intercepted the bad guys across the ditch the previous evening. If nothing else, the barking would unsettle the human prey.

After the teams had left, Sheriff Baylor had a moment to briefly inspect the scene. He was drawn to the truck sitting with its front at the bottom of the ditch and the back tires resting on the bank. As he climbed down the ditch and moved to the front, he saw the man whose body was hanging out of the windshield. The head was lying on its side, showing his face. *I'm not surprised to see this guy here. I'm sure he's the guy that went by the name Beast. He was recently paroled. I knew I'd be seeing this guy again. He was probably the ring leader. Looked like he must have thought he was too tough to need a seatbelt,* Sheriff Baylor thought as he chuckled quietly to himself.

———

As did everyone, Kent had heard the approaching patrol cars. He knew that Cal had been successful; otherwise the cavalry wouldn't be coming in for the rescue. However, he was desperate to find out how his brother was. First he had to make sure that everyone remained in their position until it was confirmed that it was safe to come in. He worked his way from position to position, asking everyone to remain in their positions until the all-clear alarm was sounded. After making the rounds, he joined John, who had walked out front worried about his wife. They both walked down to the gate together. What a welcome sight it was as they approached the gate to see Sheriff Baylor who was examining the wrecked truck and the lifeless body of its sole remaining occupant.

As the state highway patrol; the sheriff's men; the guards;

the cook; and John's wife and the dogs systematically swept up the bad guys, Kent filled in the sheriff on all that had taken place during the last twenty-four hours. He retrieved the camera from the guard shack and showed him the pictures. Sheriff Baylor recognized the man holding the gun that killed Paul. It was Beast, the same man now hanging out of the truck's windshield. The sheriff also recognized several other men in the pictures. He wasn't particularly surprised by those pictured, as he had previously dealt with them in an official capacity on one or more occasions. As they walked to the guard shack, they came to Paul's body. Sheriff Baylor removed his head gear and placed it over his heart in respect. Kent and John stood somberly by. Moments of silence passed until Sheriff Baylor spoke, extending his heartfelt sympathy.

He then said, "Unlike when Mrs. Davidson passed away, Paul will have to be taken to the coroner's office. They'll contact you when Paul's remains can be released."

After finishing up at the guard shack, the sheriff, Kent, and John went up to the lodge. Kent took the sheriff to his office and began making a formal statement. Before starting, Kent let the sheriff know that they had all been fearful of what would happen once the sun came up until they had heard the sound of the patrol cars. Kent then gave a blow by blow account of all that had transpired as Sheriff Baylor took notes. When it came to the part about the machine gun fire, Kent assured Sheriff Baylor that Paul had a license for the weapon. The license was kept in the ammo box and that he, Kent, hadn't known about it until yesterday.

Kent then asked Sheriff Baylor, "What should we do? No one else currently has a license for the machine gun."

Sheriff Baylor said, "What machine gun?"

Kent was a little slow on the uptake and responded, "The one overlooking the main gate."

Sheriff Baylor looked Kent in the eye, winked, and said, "Like I said, what machine gun?"

"Got it." Kent would make sure that someone quickly acquired a license for the weapon so that it could be a legal part of Haven's arsenal.

After Sheriff Baylor finished getting Kent's statement, he took statements from JM, the farmhand, and finally, would get the guards when they returned. He would get Cal's statement later. When he was finished, he asked Kent if he thought that Miss Sarah would be up to seeing him so he could extend his condolences to her. Kent indicated that he thought so, so they went to the area of the lodge where she was still looking after his dad.

With his hat held at his heart Sheriff Baylor approached and said, "Miss Sarah, I heard about what all has happened here. I just wanted to tell you how sorry I am about Paul. I also wanted to tell you what a brave man he was in what he did yesterday to keep the rest of you safe."

Sarah wiped the corner of her shirtsleeve to the outside edge of her eyes and replied, "Thank you, Sheriff. I know. My husband was a special guy, brave and thoughtful of the needs of others. Everyone here meant the world to him, as they do to me."

Sheriff Baylor didn't think that it would be proper to linger, so he made a couple of brief comments and went back to where Kent had been waiting. "Kent, I know I sent a card, but I want to tell you how sorry I was to hear that your mother passed away."

"She's in a better place," Kent said not wanting to elaborate for fear of breaking down in front of the sheriff.

Kent and Sheriff Baylor stepped out to the front of the lodge. Sheriff Baylor received calls on his handheld radio indicating that the immediate area was secure. They still had a couple of unidentified stragglers to pick up between the far side of the ridgeline and the main road. It shouldn't be long now he hoped. Sheriff Baylor passed the word on to Kent, who then sounded the all-clear. He asked John to arrange for a couple of people to be placed on roving patrols together after they had eaten and to make sure that the patrol was replaced regularly.

Bone Crusher had overtaken Tad as they both tried to elude the people that were searching for them. Bone Crusher heard the helicopter. He looked up and saw a helicopter from a news station out of Charlotte. They were obviously getting film footage for the next news broadcast. *If they know where I am, the cops know where I am,* Bone Crusher thought to himself.

As Bone Crusher approached him, Tad was afraid what he might do. Tad didn't say a word.

"They can see us," Bone Crusher yelled to Tad over the whooshing sound of the helicopter as he pointed up. We need to get under the trees where they can't see us." Tad nodded. "Let's go down that way," Bone Crusher said as he pointed beyond where the ridge crested. "We can work our way down off the mountain, and they won't be able to see." Again Tad nodded. "Okay, go. I'll follow along behind," Bone Crusher lied.

"Okay," Tad hollered back as he began to move at a brisk pace in the direction Bone Crusher had pointed.

Bone Crusher followed at a more leisurely pace in the same direction. As he entered into the tree line and underneath the protective cover of the canopy, he stopped. He positioned himself opposite the helicopter next to the trunk of a large tree. Bone Crusher hoped that the helicopter would follow Tad down the slope.

As soon as the helicopter had moved a short distance away, Bone Crusher carefully started moving up the slope in the opposite direction Tad was heading. Continuing the forward movement became difficult as he continued to climb. Bone Crusher had spent too much time sitting on a stool in the local bar and had let himself get out of shape. Despite his intimidating presence, he didn't have the endurance for this. *Keep moving*, he kept telling himself.

Tad was less crafty as he worked on making his getaway. He inadvertently allowed himself to be spotted by the helicopter from time to time.

"Suspect coming your way, one hundred yards south of your position, car seventeen," The pilot could see the number clearly on the top of the vehicle. He called out to the law enforcement officers below. "I say again, suspect coming your way, one hundred yards south of your position, car seventeen."

"Roger that," one of the officer's in vehicle seventeen replied.

The two officers quickly moved a hundred yards south down the road and took up concealed defensive positions. Their vehicle was beyond a bend in the road and wouldn't be visible if the suspect came as the pilot thought he would. They quietly waited for the quarry.

Tad saw the road below and stopped. He stood motionless for a moment looking in both directions to see if there was any sign of danger before continuing. All was quiet, so he slowly moved toward the road. He had no intentions of following the road. He'd certainly be picked up if he did that. Tad planned to cross the road and continue moving down the slope, hoping to eventually reach the outskirts of town where he could quietly blend in and get home. With some trepidation, Tad started across the road.

"Police officer, freeze," Tad heard as he reached the middle of the road. He didn't see anybody, but there was no doubt that the man was talking to him.

"Drop the gun and put your hands in the air," the officer instructed.

Tad dropped the pistol that had been burdening him and held both hands in the air.

"Kick it away."

Tad kicked the pistol away.

"On your knees."

Tad dropped to his knees.

"Now face down."

As soon as Tad was on his stomach, two men quickly approached him. One picked up the pistol as the other quickly put handcuffs on him. Tad was then led to the patrol car that was stationed just around the bend.

Higher up the mountain Bone Crusher was still climbing, hopefully to his freedom. In the last few minutes, he had started hearing dogs barking. He thought back to the experience the night before. Bone Crusher hoped that the dogs that were barking weren't tracking dogs. All he could do for now was to keep moving.

John's wife was clearly good with dogs; however, she was not in the physical condition required to continue the pursuit of the suspect. Realizing that she could go no farther she signaled for those that were with her to stop. She explained that she was beat and told the officer that Buster would continue tracking for him. The cook had joined her with Ivy, who was eager to continue the pursuit. Both Buster and Ivy were barking in excitement and pulling on their lines. After receiving a few last minute dog-handling instructions, they were again on their way up the mountain. The search party now consisted of the two dogs, the cook, and the remaining patrolman. They were all tired, but were intent on capturing the last of Haven's attackers.

Bone Crusher had to sit and rest for a few minutes. The helicopter appeared to be long gone, but the sound of the dogs was getting louder. Bone Crusher had nothing to lose. He knew they had pictures of him standing next to Beast when he shot the man near the front gate of Haven. He would be convicted, and this time there would be no getting out on parole. He would be in for life. As far as Bone Crusher was concerned, this was a life or death moment. Bone Crusher stood up and tried to find a vantage point from which he could see his pursuers. The same trees that had protected him from the helicopter were now working against him in finding out what he was up against.

As he reached a place that leveled off a bit, Bone Crusher moved quickly across the even terrain looking for a creek. If he could find one he could wade through, the water would cause the dogs to lose his scent, improving his chances of getting away. He could see a creek bed a little ways ahead. When he reached it, it turned out to be dry. He kept looking. Oftentimes when he had wandered in these mountains, he had to frequently ford streams to continue hunting. Bone Crusher enjoyed hunting in season or out. The forests were so vast that he knew the chances of getting caught and charged for poaching were slim. *Where's a good stream when you need one?* he thought to himself.

The search team had slowed their pace slightly, hoping to conserve enough strength to successfully apprehend the suspect. The cook would have liked to gun the thug down as soon as they saw him. He was outraged that someone would attack their peaceful Christian community and kill Paul of all people. In one moment they had taken a man's life and made his wife a widow. The cook took satisfaction in knowing that God would ultimately judge this man for what he had done.

As they continued, the dogs excitement seemed to be growing. Bone Crusher had been losing ground in this chase and knew it. There was no way he could continue at this rate so he holed up in a place that would make for an ideal ambush. Bone Crusher still had the sawed off shotgun so he'd have to let them get in close before taking out the dogs and search party. He knew he only had seven shots. He'd have to make every one count.

With the dogs in an extreme state of excitement, the officer sensed that they were close. He also recognized this as the type of place he would set up for an ambush, so he called the group to a halt. With only two people and two dogs, there was no way to surround the area. Also, the cook didn't have a weapon. It was one pistol and two dogs against whatever the suspect had. He tried calling to report the situation, but was unable to get through because of the terrain. As he was putting the radio back in its holder Buster again pulled at the line. This time it slipped out of the officer's hand, and Buster was off and running. Knowing the dog would probably be killed if this was an ambush like he suspected, the officer made a snap decision and instructed the cook to let Ivy off her line as well. When he did, Ivy shot out in the same direction.

He could hear them coming. He saw the dogs enter the area he had chosen to make his last stand. Unfortunately for Bone Crusher, a downed tree and some brush obscured his view and field of fire. He could see the hound closing in on him, held up the shotgun, and pulled the trigger.

The cook and officer heard the gun shot immediately followed by a dog yelp. The officer was afraid that he'd made the wrong decision with the dogs and would have to explain to the lady that had trained them what had happened and that he was responsible. The good thing that came from this was that they definitely knew where the suspect was located. They then heard another gun shot.

Thinking he had killed the hound dog, Bone Crusher took aim on the other dog he saw bounding toward him. He again raised his shotgun. In his fear of the dog, Bone Crusher accidently caught his foot on some underbrush and fell backwards as he pulled the trigger sending shot straight up into the air. As he hit the ground, Ivy was moving in fast. Bone Crusher raised his right arm out in front of him and across his face to protect himself as the dog lunged at him. Ivy took hold of his arm and started jerking vigorously back and forth. In desperate jerks, Bone Crusher tried to free his arm from the dog's grasp only adding to the damage that was being done.

The officer instructed the cook to stay well back as he went in. With gun raised, the officer entered the ambush area to see the suspect subdued and possibly in danger of having his arm chewed to shreds. "Release," the officer yelled per the instructions he'd been given by the dog trainer.

Bone Crusher was dazed by the viciousness of the attack. As soon as he felt the dog release its grip from him, Bone Crusher looked toward his shotgun with the remaining five shots. "Go for it and you're a dead man," the officer said. Bone Crusher relaxed and closed his eyes. The officer immediately moved over and quickly rolled Bone Crusher over placing the handcuffs on him. Bloody arm or not, the officer was not going to take a chance.

As the officer was taking care of Bone Crusher, the cook quickly moved over to Buster who was yipping.

"How's the dog?" the officer called out.

The cook bent down and could see some blood coming from Buster's upper shoulder. "It looks like he only took a pellet. He's bleeding slightly, but I think he'll be okay with some doctoring."

"I'm glad to hear that," the officer said. "Do what you can for the dog and then have a seat. I'd like to rest for about five minutes before heading back. I need to catch my breath."

"I need to be airlifted out," Bone Crusher said. As he continued, he turned slightly away from the officer so that his injured arm could be clearly seen, "Look at my arm," he said.

"Pity," the officer said. After a pause he said, "You'll be going back the way you came, on your own two feet."

"You ready to start back?" the officer asked the cook a few minutes later.

"Let's go," the cook replied. "The trip back'll be easier than the trip up," he replied.

After things settled down in Haven, JM made a point to find out where Cal and Rosebud were. Sheriff Baylor told him that Cal was at Preacher's resting up. With the road blown, JM couldn't go and get Cal and Rosebud right away. He'd have to fill in a wide enough place in the ditch to drive his truck and trailer across. JM went over to the equipment shed and got the tractor with the front-end loader and quickly got to work making a way over the ditch. He had to shift the road slightly since Beast's truck was still nose first in the ditch where the road originally had been.

With that portion of the ditch filled in, JM put the tractor away. He then hooked up the stock trailer to his pickup and left for town. When he arrived at Preacher's house, he parked out front, walked up, and knocked lightly on the front door. Preacher answered. "JM, considering all that's going on in Haven, I didn't expect to see anyone come so soon. Was anyone else hurt?" Preacher asked.

"Thankfully no, Preacher," JM replied. "When I left they'd caught all of the bad guys except two that were spotted a ways from the lodge. They should be captured soon or maybe already are."

"I was sorry to hear about Paul. I've been praying for you all ever since Cal arrived."

"Speaking of Cal, where's he at? I saw Rosebud on the way in and gave her a carrot."

"He went off to sleep. He was a sight to see when he arrived. Shall I go and get him?" Preacher asked.

"No, he deserves the rest. I can go up the street to the diner and come back later for him and Rosebud," JM said.

"I won't hear of it. Let's go on in the kitchen. I've got a pot of freshly brewed coffee made. You hungry, JM?" Preacher asked.

"Well, actually I am, now that you mention it."

"How about a BLT sandwich?" Preacher asked.

"Sure." JM answered.

"All right then. We'll give Cal some extra time to rest up, and I'll enjoy visiting with you while we wait."

After JM finished the sandwich, he and Preacher moved into the living room and continued to visit quietly. Cal finally roused from his sleep and could hear voices in the other room. He recognized JM's voice. Cal was concerned that JM would be upset with him for not following his directions more precisely. Cal got up, stopped by the bathroom on the way out, and washed his face. As he walked into the living room, JM stood and walked toward him with a big smile on his face. "I'm so thankful that you made it,"

"How'd everything turn out? Is everybody okay?" Cal asked.

"You saved the day, Cal," JM assured him.

"I thought you might be upset because I didn't follow your plans exactly like you gave them," Cal said.

"It would have gone a lot worse had you stayed with the original plan. Help wouldn't have arrived until the afternoon. There would probably have been a lot of killing done between sun up and noon."

While he listened to the conversation, Preacher thought, *We've been fortunate. It seems that God truly has been looking down on us during this tragic event.*

"You ready to head back?" As JM asked, they could all clearly hear Rosebud braying outside. "I guess Rosebud is," JM added as they all laughed.

"Preacher, thank you for your hospitality," Cal said.

"I'm honored that you thought of me in your time of need, Cal. It was my pleasure."

After they were all outside, JM loaded Rosebud onto the trailer. She didn't need any encouragement. Rosebud knew that she was going home. As they pulled away from the curb, Cal rolled the window down and hollered out to Preacher, "Thanks again."

CHAPTER ELEVEN

While JM was away picking up Cal and Rosebud, the deputies had finished apprehending the last of the thugs that had attacked Haven. The attackers that had been captured had been transported to the station for booking and questioning. The last two to be caught were Bone Crusher and Tad. Sheriff Baylor didn't want to delay the questioning of these men, so under heavy guard, they were taken to the lodge for questioning. Kent had agreed to let the sheriff use two of the downstairs rooms nearest the front entrance. Naturally, the residents of Haven were asked to stay clear of that area. Tad was placed in the room adjacent to the front door. Bone Crusher was placed in the farther room. In each of the rooms, Tad and Bone Crusher were both uncomfortable sitting forward in their chairs with their hands cuffed behind their backs. The prisoners thought the handcuffs were too tight. Law enforcement didn't want to take any chances with these dangerous men. Each prisoner had two armed officers keeping guard over them.

Shortly after being seated in the room, a half a dozen patrolmen accompanied Sarah into the room that Bone Crusher was waiting in so that she could apply first aid to his mangled arm. As they were taking the handcuffs off, Bone Crusher began to speak, but was abruptly cut off by one of the officers, "Keep your trap shut," he ordered. Sarah shrank back as the command was given. After it looked safe to proceed, Sarah sterilized and dressed the wound. Sarah would just as soon have put a knife into the man's heart as payment for the murder of her husband. However, in the depths of her soul she knew that justice did not belong to her; God would take care of this man. Leaning on her faith and strengthened by God she ministered to the criminal's wounds as she would anyone that would have come into an emergency room she might have worked in. Once she completed her duty, she left the room. The officers then placed the handcuffs back on the prisoner.

While Bone Crusher and Tad waited to be questioned, Sheriff Baylor and Kent talked about how the questioning would proceed. Sheriff Baylor asked Kent to make enlarged copies of the photos that had been taken by the guard. Sheriff Baylor agreed that Kent could be present in the room during the questioning, but was not to participate. Kent agreed and they both entered into the room where Bone Crusher was to be questioned. Sheriff Baylor began the interrogation.

As Sheriff Baylor entered the room he placed a tape recorder on the table in front of Bone Crusher and turned it on to record. "I know you've been read your rights," Sheriff Baylor said. "I'd like to ask you some questions about what went on here today."

"Not without my lawyer," Bone Crusher stated in a hateful voice.

Sheriff Baylor laid a picture on the table in front of Bone Crusher that showed him and Tad standing next to Beast, who was pointing a rifle at Paul as Paul walked away. The sheriff then laid down two additional pictures that showed the shot being taken and Paul in a motion falling forward, and the last in the series showing Paul face down in the dirt with Beast handing the rifle to Bone Crusher who had a look of satisfaction on his face in the picture. "You know this makes you an accomplice to murder," Sheriff Baylor said as he leaned toward Bone Crusher.

"Like I said, I'm not sayin' nothin' without a lawyer."

Sheriff Baylor looked toward the two that were guarding the prisoner and said, "Boys, take him in. There's nothing to be accomplished with him here."

The guards had Bone Crusher stand and marched him down the hall past the open door to the room where Tad sat. Tad saw Bone Crusher walk by. *I wonder why he didn't look in?* Tad thought. Tad then heard the front door to the lodge shut. A moment later he heard a shot ring out, directly outside. Tad jerked around to look out the window and see what had happened but was stopped by the guard before he was able to do so. At that same moment, Sheriff Baylor and Kent entered the room. Tad started to jump up and screamed, "What happened to Bone Crusher?" The guards pushed him back down in the chair.

"He wasn't useful," Sheriff Baylor replied as he placed the tape recorder on the table and turned it on to start recording. "He asked for a lawyer, so there was no point in continuing with him." As Sheriff Baylor spoke, Kent was placing the pictures that Sheriff Baylor had shown to Bone Crusher down one-by-one on the table. Then the sheriff asked, "So, do you want a lawyer?"

"No, I don't want one," Tad demanded. "What do you want to know?"

"You've been read your rights. Are you waiving them now?" Sheriff Baylor asked.

"Yes, I'm waiving my rights," Tad quickly answered.

"All right then, let's begin with your name, your full name."

"Theodore Oswald Preston. I go by Tad."

"All right, Tad. What was your part in all of this?"

"My brother made me come," Tad answered. "I didn't want to come, but I was afraid of him."

"Who is your brother? You said you were afraid of him. You're not afraid of him now?" Sheriff Baylor asked.

"He died in the truck. His head went through the windshield."

"And your brother's name?"

"Patrick Preston, but people just called him Beast," Tad answered.

"Who decided to come here and why?" Sheriff Baylor asked.

"My brother did. When he got out of prison, someone told him that this would be an easy place to make some money."

"How would they make money here?" Sheriff Baylor asked.

"He didn't say exactly. I think maybe someone was going to give him money, but he never came right out and said it," Tad explained.

"Who would give him money?" Sheriff Baylor demanded.

"I don't know. He never said," Tad replied convincingly.

"So let me get this straight. Your brother makes you come along and attack some people so that he might get paid some money?"

"That's right," Tad said. "But there's more."

"Go ahead," Sheriff Baylor said.

"My brother had a sketch of the place showing where the antenna for the radio was. That's how we knew to knock it out before coming."

"Where's the sketch now?" Sheriff Baylor asked, hoping

that it would provide a clue as to who might be behind the attack.

"He burned it up last night since he didn't need it anymore," Tad answered.

"Did you see it?"

"Not really. I saw the paper, but he didn't let me look at the sketch," Tad answered. "That's just how he was."

"And the phone lines, who took care of that?" Sheriff Baylor asked.

"I don't know anything about the phone lines. He just said it was taken care of."

Over 500 miles away just outside the nation's capital, Senator Bailey Beauregard Bates had gone home for the night and retired to his den. He sat in an overstuffed leather chair in a room that screamed, "I am important." He had poured himself a cognac that he sat on the end table next to him, lit a cigar, and picked up the afternoon newspaper. After reading the headlines of the front page, he reached over and turned on the news. He listened as he scanned the paper. When the reporter started talking about an attack on the community of Haven in the western part of North Carolina B. B. tossed the paper on the floor next to his chair, leaned over, and gave the reporter his full attention.

"... aerial footage of the place where the attack took place." B. B. could clearly see a truck nose first in a ditch with what looked like a body protruding from the windshield. "Reports coming in indicate that a lone rider braved the forested mountain under the cover of darkness on the back of a mule and rode for help, all communication lines having been severed." The camera then moved over to a lodge. "... Alleged attackers are being questioned in this mysterious attack on this mysterious community. We cannot yet report on the nature of the community. More information will be provided as this story develops. Stay tuned for continuing updates."

B. B. punched the remote turning the TV off. He wanted to call Alexander but thought it might not be a good idea to have a record of a phone call being placed from his home or personal cell phone to him should tracks start leading back to him.

Agent Booker happened to have the news turned on and heard the same broadcast. He immediately began to worry about his part in the attack coming out in the open. Agent Booker didn't think it would take a lot to convince a common criminal to give his name as the source of the sketch showing where the antenna was located that had to be taken out. He had made sure not to send it from his office or from anywhere that could be traced back to him. The guard he knew at the prison that gave him Beast's name probably wouldn't be a problem. He had enough on him to keep him quiet, and Beast wouldn't know about the guard's involvement anyway. All he could do now was hunker down and hope nothing came up that would lead in his direction.

"Then how did the phone lines get cut," Sheriff Baylor asked.

"I don't know. Really, I don't know," Tad pleaded hoping not to have the same fate as Bone Crusher and his brother, Beast.

"So, what else do you know about the sketch. Who made it? You've got to know something," Sheriff Baylor continued.

"Oh yes, I remember he said something about an IRS man," Tad added.

This last comment made Kent think about what his brother had said about B. B. having some kind of connection with someone in the IRS in North Carolina. *Is there a connection between the IRS agent that B. B. knows and the IRS person that this guy's talking about or is this just a coincidence?* Kent wondered. *And how about Agent Booker?* In confidence Kent shared with Sheriff Baylor about the conversation he'd recently had with his brother, even though none of what Brad had told him could be substantiated.

"Who was the IRS guy you're talking about? I need a name," Sheriff Baylor demanded.

"I swear to you, I never heard a name. In fact, I don't know that my brother ever knew the actual name of the person he was dealing with."

Sheriff Baylor instructed the men that were guarding the prisoner to take him in for booking. He figured he'd gotten about all he was going to get here. Kent followed Sheriff Baylor out of the room. They went up to Kent's office to discuss what they had learned.

As Tad exited the lodge, he was led to a waiting patrol car with Bone Crusher sitting in the back seat. Tad couldn't believe what he was seeing. He was sure they had shot Bone Crusher out of revenge for the killing of one of their people. One of the officers opened the door and placed Tad next to Bone Crusher.

"Did you keep your trap shut?" Bone Crusher asked in an accusing manner.

"Yeah, I didn't say a thing," Tad lied. Tad was hoping that he'd be placed in a separate cell from Bone Crusher. He actually hoped that he would never see him again.

"So what took you so long?" Bone Crusher asked.

"I don't know," Tad said as if he had no idea in the world. "They had me sitting in there for a long time. It was just me and the guards most of the time. I don't know why it took so long."

Bone Crusher leaned over and quietly said in Tad's ear, "If you talked, you're a dead man."

Tad deliberately turned his head away from Bone Crusher, hoping that his face didn't betray him. They sat in silence after the officer got in the car and drove them to the police station to be booked. Bone Crusher hoped he would get a good public defender that would get him the shortest sentence possible. There was no way he was going to wiggle out of this with them having those pictures.

As Sheriff Baylor and Kent were discussing what the men had said, Cal entered Kent's office. Kent quickly got up and walked over to his brother giving him a big hug. "I've already thanked God for your safe journey last night. If it wasn't for what you did Cal," Kent paused a moment holding back the emotion he felt, "I hate to think about what would have happened."

"I told you I'd make it, Kent," Cal told his brother.

Sheriff Baylor walked over to Cal, reached over, and shook Cal's hand. "Congratulations on a job well done. Your brother here told me about your brave actions last night."

"Somebody had to go for help," Cal replied.

"Apparently, you were the right man for the job," Sheriff Baylor answered.

Agent Booker's phone rang. It was Senator Bates. The senator gave him a phone number and instructed him to call him there in an hour from a pay phone. Agent Booker left his office, got in his car, and drove until the hour was nearly up. He stopped at a grocery store and got a couple of rolls of quarters. He then drove around until he found a pay phone and dialed the number. He heard the phone ringing.

"Alexander, what can you tell me about what's going on in Haven?"

"Even though the attack wasn't completely successful, there is some good news," Agent Booker offered.

"I could use some good news," the senator replied.

"The good news is that the criminal I coordinated the attack with died in the attack. As long as he followed my instructions and didn't share the details with any of his companions and destroyed the sketch of Haven as I instructed him, there's no way that any of this can be traced..." Agent Booker let the sentence hang for a moment. He instinctively was going to say *back to us,* but finished by saying, "...back to me." Agent Booker figured the Senator would realize on his own that if he went down he'd take the Senator down with him.

"I certainly hope that your suppositions are well founded, Alexander. I think it would be best to cease and desist on any other actions aimed at Haven for now. In the meantime I think it would be productive to do a little research and identify people that are no longer paying taxes and see if you can track them to a community like Haven. We can work on putting the pressure on other new self-sustained communities that are starting to spring up."

"I'll get on it, Senator," Agent Booker replied, looking forward to bringing this conversation to a close.

"Stay in touch, Alexander. Let me know if anything happens regarding Haven."

"You can count on it, Senator Bates," Agent Booker answered.

Agent Booker heard, "Okay," followed by a click on the other end.

As Kent, Cal, and Sheriff Baylor were discussing the day's events, one of the farmhands tapped on the doorframe that led into the office. "Come on in," Kent instructed.

The farmhand looked at Kent and glanced at the others. "I thought you all would want to know that the phone line's working again.

"What was the problem?" Kent asked.

"As we had suspected, the phone line was cut."

"Where was the line cut at?" Kent asked.

"Below the exterior phone box at the back of the lodge. The line was cut just below ground level," the farmhand explained.

"Thanks," Kent replied as the farmhand turned to go back to his work.

"That raises a whole new dimension to the attack," Sheriff Baylor said.

"How so?" Cal asked.

"Had to have been an inside job," Kent answered. He then turned and looked at the sheriff. "That's what you meant, isn't it?"

"Exactly," Sheriff Baylor answered. "I can't think of any other explanation. Are there any of your residents that you'd be suspicious of?" he asked.

"We don't really know everybody yet, sheriff," Kent answered. "Some of the people that came we knew from before, but there are a few that are new to us. I wouldn't know where to start."

"How about you, Cal?" Sheriff Baylor asked. "Do you have any ideas about who would do something like this?"

"Not really," Cal answered.

"Have either of you seen any suspicious activity among any of the residents?" Kent and Cal both shook their heads.

"Can you think of anything that was even remotely out of the ordinary?" Sheriff Baylor asked.

"I can think of one incident now that you mention it, but I didn't think anything of it at the time," Cal said. "Mr. Rivera was behind the lodge one day near the storage area. I asked him why he was there. He said he wanted to know where to go if he needed anything later."

"That doesn't sound particularly damaging," Sheriff Baylor said. "But how about we have a few words with him and see how he responds?"

Cal said, "No problem, I'll go and get him."

"Hold up just a minute, Cal," Sheriff Baylor said. "We need to have a plan. We need to put him at ease. It might be best if I wasn't in the room because that could make him tense and not say anything if there's anything to say."

"All right, sheriff. I could have Cal ask Mr. Rivera to come up and talk to me privately," Kent said. "Sheriff, would you please wait in John's office until I finish or need to call you in?"

"Okay, I'll be next door. Since the phones are working now I'll call in and see if they've learned anything from the other prisoners."

"I'll go and get Mr. Rivera, Kent," Cal said. "Once he's in your office, I'll join Sheriff Baylor next door."

"I'll be waiting here for Mr. Rivera."

Cal found Mr. Rivera and a couple of other men in the dining area drinking coffee. Cal approached him and said in a matter-of-fact manner, "Kent would like to see you in his office if it's convenient."

"Sure, I'll go right up," Mr. Rivera said in an equally matter-of-fact manner. Mr. Rivera wondered, *Have they found out already?* He left the others and walked up the stairs and then down the hall to Kent's office. Kent saw him coming and motioned him in. "You called for me?" Mr. Rivera asked.

"Yes, come on in. Have a seat. I just wanted to visit with

you for a few minutes." Mr. Rivera was suspicious about the timing of this visit. As Mr. Rivera sat quietly in front of him, Kent continued, "This has been a tragic time for our community, and I wanted to check with everyone to make sure they're doing all right. You know, when things like Paul's murder take place, a lot of people need counseling. How is your family doing?" Kent asked.

"We're all pretty upset that something like this would happen here in Haven. Everyone up here is so nice. I don't know why anyone would come up here and bother us." Mr. Rivera was sincere in what he had said. "I know people are being attacked all over the country. Neighbor attacking neighbor for their food. Terrorists bombing shopping malls and other easy targets for no reason that I can understand."

"I'm sure you know that the antenna was neutralized and the phone lines cut before the actual attack," Kent said.

"Yes, I heard that," Mr. Rivera answered.

We've already discovered that the phone line was cut right behind the lodge. The attackers didn't have access to that area so we believe that the line being severed was an inside job," Kent explained.

"Oh my," Mr. Rivera said.

"Do you know anybody that would want to do that to us here?" Kent asked.

"I can honestly tell you I don't. I don't know anybody that would want to do that." Mr. Rivera knew that he didn't want to do it, but he had to. Agent Booker had threatened ruining his brother's life if he didn't cut that phone line. He honestly didn't know anybody that would want to do it. But if he exposed what he knew about this whole matter he could be charged as an accomplice to murder. He wanted to tell Kent the whole truth, but couldn't take the chance. He'd pray for God's forgiveness. He just wouldn't be able to ask for forgiveness from Paul's wife or from the others here in Haven.

It felt to Kent like Mr. Rivera was being honest with him. He ended the conversation by saying, "If there's anything your family needs to help you get through this situation, please let me know."

"Thank you for your kindness," Mr. Rivera said as he left Kent's office ashamed of his part in what had happened.

After Mr. Rivera had gone down the stairs, Kent called his brother and Sheriff Baylor back into his office and told them about the conversation.

"Well, we had to give it a try," Sheriff Baylor said. "So it was a dead end."

The following day, Cal had some help getting the antenna back into operation. The line had been cut, but fortunately the antenna was still fully functional once it was reconnected. Even though the radio hadn't been able to help in this emergency some of the men saw the potential and were interested in learning how to operate it. They were concerned about not being able to learn Morse code. Cal then explained to them that they didn't need anything to be qualified to use the forty-channel CB Radio. He also explained how they could qualify to use the shortwave radio and that being proficient in Morse code was no longer a requirement. Cal thought it was nice that a few guys were showing an interest in getting more involved in Haven.

The following morning Sheriff Baylor proceeded to interrogate Bone Crusher and the other prisoners that had been a part of the attack on Haven. Before beginning he made sure that Bone Crusher had the opportunity to have an attorney present. Bone Crusher and his attorney were waiting in the interrogation room when Sheriff Baylor entered. He took note of the extensive bandages the accused had on his right arm. It was little consolation considering that Paul had been killed and Sarah left a widow.

Sheriff Baylor then placed the photos down on the table one by one in clear view of both Bone Crusher and his attorney. He then placed the tape recorder on the table and punched the record button. The room had a built in recorder. The machine was used as a psychological tool. Sheriff Baylor wanted the accused to have no doubt that this interrogation was a serious matter with potentially serious consequences. "I'm sure you can see your client was having quite a time yesterday," Sheriff Baylor said to Bone Crusher's attorney who looked disinterested in what had just been said. Turning to Bone Crusher Sheriff Baylor said, "This will all go easier on you if you'll cooperate."

Bone Crusher knew that he couldn't beat the system this time. He had gotten off with suspended sentences for his earlier crimes from his past. Later he started getting some jail time. Most recently he had been a guest in the state pen. Bone Crusher also realized that he didn't have any information that would be useful, something to use in exchange for a lighter sentence.

"Where did the information come from that you used to attack Haven?" Sheriff Baylor asked. Bone Crusher straightened up in his chair, leaned toward Sheriff Baylor as if he might have something important to say, and then spit in his face.

Acting in a calm manner, as if nothing had happened, Sheriff Baylor picked up the photos, mashed the off button, picked up the tape recorder, turned, and walked out the door. The interrogation was over. Sheriff Baylor had not been hopeful that he would learn anything from this criminal. He had suspected that Tad was telling the truth about what he knew. That being the case there was nothing that could have been learned here anyway.

By the time Sheriff Baylor had concluded the interrogations, he was convinced that Tad had known more than anybody about what was going to take place in Haven, and that wasn't much. With what information he had, he scheduled an appointment with the district attorney to discuss the case. After sharing all he knew with the DA, Sheriff Baylor had been told that he would have to be satisfied with finding justice for the men he already had in custody. Sheriff Baylor had made an impassioned argument to seek subpoenas for phone records for the IRS agent that had audited Haven and for Senator Bailey Beauregard Bates. The sheriff had even told the DA in confidence about what Kent's brother had told him concerning the phone conversation they had shared. As much as the DA would have liked to get down to the bottom of any wrongdoing that might have been behind the attack, he wasn't willing to jeopardize the reputation of his office or his own reputation as an attorney. There was too much at stake.

After his meeting with the DA, Sheriff Baylor went to Haven. He wanted to talk frankly with Kent, man to man. When he arrived, he went directly to Kent's office. As the sheriff entered, Kent stood and greeted him. "How's your investigation going sheriff?" Kent asked.

"Not as well as I would have liked," Sheriff Baylor responded. "Oh, we've got the guys that attacked you. There's no way they're going to weasel out of this one. The fact that Paul was murdered will make the sentences longer for everyone involved."

"So, what's the problem?" Kent asked.

"The people that were really behind this attack are going to get away with whatever their involvement was. That's what gets me. That's why I came here this afternoon. I wanted to tell you myself. I came here directly from the DA's office. He's not going to initiate an investigation to try and get to the bottom of this."

"I'm not surprised," Kent said. "If it is a prominently placed person in the IRS and a United States Senator, this would be huge. Maybe not as big as Watergate, but huge."

"Knowing what we do, you'll need to continually watch your back, Kent, you and your entire community. It sounds like, somehow, you've managed to make enemies in high places."

"Sheriff, I've tried to live my live in accordance with Christian principals. I do the best I can to treat everyone fairly. It's hard to understand why one or more people would go out of their way to hurt us. I don't see what could possibly be in it for them."

"That puzzles me too, Kent," Sheriff Baylor replied. "Well, that's really all I came over to say. I'm sorry I couldn't do more."

"You saved the day for us yesterday," Kent said. "Thank you for that."

"Thank your brother Cal," Sheriff Baylor said. "He was the real hero yesterday. I'll keep you in the loop if I learn anything more."

"Would you like to stay and have dinner with us?" Kent asked.

"As much as I'd like to, my wife is expecting me home in a little bit. I've got to get going. Thanks for the offer though."

"We'll leave it as a standing invitation. Bring your wife with you sometime. Thanks again."

As he left Kent's office, Sheriff Baylor was sad that he wasn't able to do more.

A week later, a funeral was conducted for Paul. It was a graveside service at the cemetery behind the farmhouse where Kent's mother had been laid to rest. Both of Paul and Sarah's sons were granted emergency leave, were on hand, and sat with their mother during the funeral. Preacher officiated. Most of the in-town congregation of Preacher's church came to join the residents of Haven. Also present was a funeral detail from the United States Army to provide full military honors in recognition of Paul's years of honorable military service. Kent gave the eulogy, recognizing many of the military accomplishments Paul had rendered to his country. He also mentioned the selfless sacrifice that Paul had made in the company of his wife, Sarah, in making Haven what it is today. Paul was an example of what a Christian should be in all that he did. After the eulogy, there was a fifteen-gun salute followed by the folding of the flag that had been draped across his casket.

The officer in charge then knelt down before Sarah and said, "Ma'am, this flag is presented on behalf of a grateful nation and the United States Army, as a token of appreciation for your loved one's honorable and faithful service." He then stood, saluted the flag that now lay in Sarah's lap, and returned to his post.

Preacher ended the service.

After the funeral, everyone went to the dining room to join in an additional time of remembrance. Standing off to the side, Kent turned his head toward Sheriff Baylor and somberly said, "I don't know how our government could ever consider retirees such as Paul a security threat to our nation. It's a shame that duty, honor, and country are something that our elected representatives don't adopt as a part of their life. They would do well to emulate men such as Paul."

"I know what you mean. It's hard to understand most of what comes out of Washington anymore," Sheriff Baylor replied.

At home for the weekend, Senator Bates was reclining in his favorite easy chair reading the Washington Post. He had his usual glass of cognac on the end table next to him and a lit cigar that had been resting on the crystal ashtray beside it. He was basking in the satisfaction of the passing of his most recent pork barrel spending legislation that would bring a lot of money to North Carolina and his most trusted colleagues' states. The phone rang. *That should be Alexander now,* Senator Bates thought to himself.

"It's me," Agent Booker said.

"Alexander, what a pleasure to hear your voice. It will be even better if you've got some good news this time."

"Senator, I'm pleased to tell you that my man in the DA's office assures me that there will be no further investigation." Agent Booker had become more cautious about saying anything more incriminating than was necessary. He knew that Senator Bates felt the same.

"Excellent, Alexander, excellent. How about that other matter we discussed previously?"

"Oh that," Agent Booker answered. "Yes, I've been looking into it. I did some searching of records as you suggested and found some inconsistencies in taxes being paid by numerous people, many of which are retired military and other retired government servants. I'm in the process of determining if they too have ventured into a clandestine lifestyle thinking they will be free from paying any more taxes than they have to."

"I'm glad to hear you are making progress. I also wanted to ask, have you come up with any strategy to take care of the root of the problem in the self-sustained community world?"

Agent Booker had had a brainstorm one evening thinking about the children that lived in Haven. He wasn't yet ready to share the details with Senator Bates. "I think I've got a possible strategy, but I've got to do my homework. I'm seeing if I can come up with something with my point of contact at the Department of Human Services. If anything comes of it, I'll fill you in on the details."

"Stay in touch, Alexander," Senator Bates said as he hung

up the phone and turned to the mail that sat on the end table next to his cognac. One piece of mail in particular caught his attention; it didn't have a return address, but was postmarked from the state of North Carolina. He opened it and found a card that said, "Thinking of you," on the cover. He opened the card. There was no note. It was merely signed, "Kent Davidson."

The day after the funeral, Cal spent the day working in the storage area trying to catch back up. A lot of things had gone by the wayside during the last week. Later in the afternoon, Cal took a break and went back to the mineshaft that he had focused his prospecting in. After working a few minutes, he picked up a rock that had fallen to the ground as it had caught his attention. It seemed kind of heavy for its size. He gently tossed it up and down in the palm of his right hand. "Well now, what have we got here?" he asked himself.

listen|imagine|view|experience

AUDIO BOOK DOWNLOAD INCLUDED WITH THIS BOOK!

In your hands you hold a complete digital entertainment package. In addition to the paper version, you receive a free download of the audio version of this book. Simply use the code listed below when visiting our website. Once downloaded to your computer, you can listen to the book through your computer's speakers, burn it to an audio CD or save the file to your portable music device (such as Apple's popular iPod) and listen on the go!

How to get your free audio book digital download:

1. Visit www.tatepublishing.com and click on the e|LIVE logo on the home page.
2. Enter the following coupon code:
   ece0-cba0-7098-70ad-2aec-8448-4a72-31b9
3. Download the audio book from your e|LIVE digital locker and begin enjoying your new digital entertainment package today!